BAUER

The K9 Files, Book 22

Dale Mayer

BAUER: THE K9 FILES, BOOK 22
Beverly Dale Mayer
Valley Publishing Ltd.

Copyright © 2023

ISBN-13: 978-1-773367-56-9
Print Edition

Books in This Series

About This Book

Welcome to the all new K9 Files series reconnecting readers with the unforgettable men from SEALs of Steel in a new series of action packed, page turning romantic suspense that fans have come to expect from USA TODAY Bestselling author Dale Mayer. Pssst... you'll meet other favorite characters from SEALs of Honor and Heroes for Hire too!

Staying in town suited Bauer. Dealing with Kat and Badger's matchmaker? Not so much. But, when a mutual friend calls to say an injured War Dog was dropped off at her clinic—only to then be stolen during the night after she completed surgery to fix his injured stump—well, Bauer is all over it.

Mags always liked Bauer, but she kept her personal relationships short and sweet. After all, commitments were too often broken and the resultant pain horrific. However, Bauer refuses to leave her in trouble and is here for her every step of the way; plus they share the love of animals. How can she ignore all that? Plus he is a hell of a package. But is she willing to take a chance on being hurt again?

The escalating danger—surrounding Toby, her injured War Dog—catches Mags and Bauer in a web of risk that can only end one way ...

Sign up to be notified of all Dale's releases here!

https://geni.us/DaleNews

PROLOGUE

KAT STARED AT Badger. "There's such a miraculous note to these endings," she whispered.

Badger nodded, his voice equally soft as he spoke, after the phone call ended. "Who would have thought that Declan would have wrapped that up so nicely. Not only a cold case on her family's murder but the attacks against Carly leading up to this, and he secured the War Dog."

Kat shook her head. "I know it's a twisted world out there, but, Dear God, that's quite a story."

"And yet here we are, doing our part to fix things."

"Declan wants to keep Shelby then?"

"Oh, I think it's probably the best answer in this case, as they get to share the dog." Badger smiled. "Shelby might do well with the hospitals too, but she will definitely do well in terms of various K9 work."

"That's huge, absolutely huge. My God." Kat gave a big sigh and placed her hand on her chest. "My heart swells, I'm so happy."

He smiled at her. "That's because you're such a good person."

She chuckled. "This has been one hell of an experience. I know we're not making any money on it, and money isn't the point, but, wow, are we ever affecting lives."

"In a good way." Badger nodded. "It's all very hard to

imagine." Then he looked down at the file in front of him. "It makes we wish we could help others, even if not through this K9 program."

"You're thinking of Timber, aren't you?" Kat smiled at her husband. "He's doing very well."

"I know he is. That man seems to be able to do anything when it comes to construction work. I did ask him if he found out more about that property he was interested in, and he said yes. And that was it. No update. No further response." Badger laughed. "I can't even consider him unfriendly, as he answered me with a smile."

"There you go. When he's ready to share, he will."

"We'll miss him, if he decides to do something other than help us."

"Maybe we should consider a construction side to our current businesses."

Badger snorted. "As if we don't have one now. Although, if Timber wanted to do something along that line, I'd support him. He really knows what he's doing."

"So maybe bring it up with him. I know he's fighting his own demons, but it never hurts to remind someone that they aren't alone." She smiled at Badger, watching as he fingered the file in front of him. "You've got another one, don't you?"

He nodded. "I do. I was wondering about Bauer."

"Not Timber? Bauer, *huh*? Wasn't he setting up a search and rescue operation around here?"

"He was thinking about it, but something holds him back. He just keeps talking about it. I've asked him to take one of these jobs over and over again, but he keeps saying no, tells me that he's not ready."

"Any reason why not?"

"Because he had a K9 dog, who saved Bauer's life, but he

lost the dog. Of course Bauer lost a leg and a hand in the deal, so overall, it left him with a bad taste for the military."

"Right, we're still working to get that one prosthetic right, but otherwise he's been doing really well."

Badger nodded. "I'd like to see him do one of these jobs and get him over the hump and to see if that kind of work is really what he wants."

"It's funny because I do remember you talking to him about this last year."

Badger smiled. "Yeah, because I know that's where his heart is, and I wanted to see if he could get past being stuck and help one of these animals."

"Does he know it's something that he needs to get through?"

"I don't know. I've talked to him a bunch of times, but—"

"Where's the dog?"

"That's another reason for it. Otherwise I'd be tempted to do it myself."

Kat looked at her husband in surprise. "Do you want a War Dog? I mean, I'm sure one of these dogs could become yours if you wanted one."

"I don't know," Badger admitted. "I've been thinking about it. I mean, you hear these stories, and you wonder."

"Oh, wait, hang on a minute. I get it. You're looking for a new woman, aren't you?"

He grinned at her. "Oh, dang, busted. Come on. Do you think you aren't more than enough woman for me? Not to mention the *kids*," he added, with an eye roll.

"Absolutely. So, come on. Tell me about this one. Then let's give Bauer a call."

"That's the thing. This War Dog is a big male, missing a

back leg. It was adopted, then he had more medical problems, and that's when they took off the leg. Then they abandoned it at the vet clinic."

"Seriously?"

He nodded.

Kat frowned. "And it's local, right? So this really isn't a search and rescue or a hunt-and-retrieve type thing."

"Not really, no, but I talked to the vet about it, and you do know the vet."

"Sure, if we're talking about Mags. Or Magrit Wilden."

"We are, indeed, talking about Mags," Badger confirmed, "and I know she's a good friend of yours, but, hey, she is single."

At that, Kat stared at him in surprise. "You're not actively matchmaking, are you?"

"No, of course not," he declared.

She rolled her eyes. "Of course you are. How else do you explain all these happy-ending K9 cases?"

"They weren't solely about matchmaking," he replied in a dry tone. "I know Bauer wants to stay local with his new job, but I thought maybe he might want to work with this dog some."

"But why did it end up in our files, if it's local and if it's already here?"

"Because, in this case, the dog doesn't have a home."

"So we're supposed to do an adoption for it? That's hardly within the scope of how we started."

"As you know, everything here that we started has kind of changed over time, but it's also because Mags phoned me this morning."

She looked at him in surprise. "When?"

"Yeah, I would have told you about it, but Declan called

when you walked in, so I haven't had a chance."

"What's the matter?"

"His name's Toby, the War Dog, I mean. Mags had a stranger come into her place yesterday, who took a real shine to the dog, and she told the guy that all the adoption information had to go through us. He apparently got really ugly about it. So, when she came in this morning, there had been a break-in, and the dog is missing."

"Ah, shit."

"So now she feels guilty as hell, and Toby is missing."

Kat stared at him. "And you're thinking Bauer is the guy for the job?"

"Bauer knows the area. Bauer knows dogs. Bauer knows Mags." Then he shot Kat a sideways look.

She stared at him for a long moment. "You know what? It just might work. Mags is pretty definite about not getting involved again, though. She says she only wants to be around animals."

"Which is also Bauer's point. He isn't in any hurry to get involved with anyone again, not after his wife walked away with his best friend while he was overseas."

Kat winced at that. "Right, I had heard that. Mags is a veterinarian, with a kind heart, who looks after animals. Then there's Bauer, who is a little bit on the rough side, yet—you know something?" Kat looked at Badger in surprise. "You're getting pretty good at this."

"Bauer hasn't said yes though."

At that came a laugh at the doorway, and they both looked up to see Bauer, leaning against the door.

"What are you two hatching now?" he asked in disgust. "It better not have anything to do with my love life."

"No, not at all," Badger replied. "Do you know the vet

here, Mags?"

He straightened. "Sure, why?"

"Her clinic got broken into this morning."

At that news, Bauer straightened and glared at Badger. "What?"

"Yeah, and the War Dog that I mentioned to you is now missing." Badger then explained what Mags had told him on the phone this morning.

"That little punk bastard isn't taking a dog that's already struggling and go out and do what with Toby? If that's how this punk treats the vet, you know he'll treat the dog like shit."

"I know, and you know what will end up happening with a guy like that."

"Yeah, the dog'll go after him, after it's taken all it can handle."

"So, Mags really needs a hand," Badger said, looking at him. "She feels terrible."

Bauer glared. "I'm heading to the vet clinic right now." He spun back to the doorway.

"So, does that mean you're taking the case?" Badger asked.

Bauer turned and asked, "What do you mean, *case?*"

"Remember? I talked to you about all these War Dogs?"

"Sure, but I wouldn't do it." Then he frowned and asked, "Is that what this is?"

Badger nodded. "It is. Mags was just checking the dog over because it was abandoned. Someone had brought it to her. When she scanned it, she realized it was a War Dog and contacted us."

"Well, hell," Bauer muttered. "Looks like you'll get your way then."

"And what does that mean? I really need you to be clear about this," Badger said.

Bauer glared at him and saw the grin on Badger's face. "Hell yes, you know I won't let a loser punk steal a War Dog like that. Besides, Mags is one hell of a vet. If she needs a hand, I'll be there." And, with that, he stormed off.

Kat looked over at her husband and smiled. "That was dirty."

"Hey, it worked, didn't it?" Badger noted, with a smile. "Now we just have to let nature take its course."

CHAPTER 1

BAUER ARMSTRONG HOPPED into his truck and headed over to the vet clinic. He got along well with Mags, but there was kind of a reserved energy between them. It was all business and nothing more, and that's the way he preferred it. Yet always this undercurrent. This awareness between them. He had a huge distrust of women in general. He knew it wasn't fair, but, when something has colored your past, it was hard to not let it color your future as well. Not being the kind of person to do a lot of self-analysis and figure it out, Bauer didn't want to even think about it because it was too painful and required way too much of that touchy-feely stuff.

He could get as emotional as the next guy, but it hurt when it came to some events in his life, and he just wasn't prepared to go there. The loss of his wife. The loss of his War Dog.

Bauer shook those thoughts from his head, as he pulled into the parking lot of the veterinary clinic. He watched a window company employee taking measurements. Bauer wandered around the outside of the clinic to see just what kind of damage had been done to the place. When one of the window guys looked at him with a raised eyebrow, Bauer shrugged. "I heard about it this morning and came by to see how bad it was."

"Went in through a window," he said. "Don't know

whether they had security on or not, but, if they did, it didn't do them much good."

That was a critical point, and something Bauer would ask Mags about, though she may not take it in the way it was intended. Still, this might shake her up too. Bauer walked back around to the front entrance of the clinic, pushed open the door, and stepped inside.

Mags stood behind the counter, going over files with her receptionist. Mags looked up and acknowledged him, with a short nod. "Hey. What can I do for you today?"

"Badger sent me over."

Her eyebrows popped up. "Why?"

That was her attitude, blunt and right to the point. She was known for not bullshitting around. He kind of liked it. He could handle anybody who was straightforward and honest. It didn't matter what the questions were, but, when people started playing games, Bauer had a tendency to get irate. "Because of the break-in and the War Dog."

"Right," Mags let out a sigh. "Don't get me started on poor Toby."

"What kind of physical condition is he in?"

"We just took off his back leg," she shared in frustration. "It's bound up, but his pain meds must be wearing off by now. The drainage and threat of infection are major concerns."

Bauer frowned at that. "And a hurt, angry dog won't be easy to control."

"No, he sure won't. Toby is pretty exceptional though. I never saw the slightest hint of aggression out of him the whole time I had him here."

"I didn't get a whole lot of history from Badger," Bauer noted. "Do you have a photo?"

She nodded, then pulled out her phone. After swiping around, she located one. "Here. He's a handsome guy, a big Malinois-shepherd cross. Other than missing his back leg and being almost totally midnight black, the only other distinguishing features are the lighter ear tufts and the matching one at end of his tail."

Bauer studied the photo. "Interesting. Any more information on file?"

"Not much at all," she replied. "Toby was found close by, and it looks as if somebody probably just dumped him here close to us, maybe so he would at least get the help he needed. Then they took off, probably so they didn't have to pay the bill, I suppose."

"I'm looking for information on the family who originally adopted him," Bauer added, "but, so far, I haven't gotten that data."

"Badger will have it," Mags stated. "Or, if he doesn't, he probably knows where to get it, at least. It would be good to know what happened on that end, but that's not today's issue. Right not, we just need to get Toby back and fast."

Bauer nodded. "Did you have the security system on?"

She nodded. "I did. I personally close up every night, especially when I have animals here."

"Were any other animals taken?"

She shook her head at that. "No," she muttered. "Toby is the only one that went missing."

"Okay, so what can you tell me about the guy who came here asking, about the dog?"

She snorted at that. "I can do one better and show you a picture from the security camera. I went looking for it first thing."

She led the way back into a small room, where the security system was set up and connected to a laptop, which she quickly accessed, bringing up the image of the man who she had been talking to the day before. "This is him." She pointed at the image. "Not the best angle to get a good look at him. He was kind of unassuming in a way, but he didn't really like anything I had to say."

"Was he aggressive? Was he difficult or threatening?"

"Things got ugly in that he got mad, yet he didn't directly threaten me. He was argumentative. On every point of the adoption process, he didn't want to hear what I had to say."

"Did it seem as if he knew the dog?"

She frowned. "I don't know about that. He certainly had heard about it, but I'd had the information out on the news media, trying to find somebody who might know what was going on with Toby."

"Right, so maybe he was ex-military and just wanted to do something."

"Maybe, though he wasn't some do-gooder, happy to help. He was no philanthropist, in my opinion. He had another motive here. Plus he didn't look like he had a whole lot of money. He didn't look like he was homeless either, by any means, but I don't know for sure." She shrugged. "I don't want to make a judgment call solely based on appearances, but let's just say, I didn't think he could afford Toby's vet bill."

"So, is that what you were looking for? Someone who could cover Toby's medical expenses?"

One eyebrow lifted, and her gaze narrowed. "No, I wasn't. In this case, I'd already taken on Toby's case as a kindness to an animal that needed help." She gave a one-arm shrug. "I can only do so many of those a year, without running into trouble myself, trying to pay *my* bills." Again she sighed. "However, in this case, no way I wouldn't help."

"Right, because it was a war animal."

She looked at him and nodded slowly. "How would you know that would make a difference to me?"

"I don't," he admitted, "but it sure makes a difference to me."

"Why?" she asked.

"Because of my own naval service. Any animal that went through even a portion of what I went through deserves as much help as it can get. Those animals worked hard and trained hard, so to think of Toby out there suffering now makes me sick."

"I get that," she agreed, "which is another reason why we were here, trying to help him."

He looked at her and frowned. "Are you sure there wasn't another reason? Are you attached to Toby already?"

She gave him a flat stare and then ignored him.

He grinned at that. "I like how you can just shut down a conversation with a glance," he admitted cheerfully.

"Apparently *not*, because you're still right here, bothering me," she said, but her tone was lighter, as if realizing that he wouldn't go away just because she wanted him to.

"You and I both know that I need to get out there and find this dog, and I need to locate him fast."

"I won't argue with that," she said. "It would be great if you could find Toby *before* all his pain meds wear off."

"Which is when?"

She glanced at her watch, grimacing. "Two hours ago." He winced and she nodded. "Considering how much pain Toby may have been in before, it's possible that he may do okay for a time without the medicine," she suggested. "Yet you and I both know what could happen when that pain kicks in to the point that he can't handle it anymore."

"I do know, and it's the same for any animal. He'll try to run. He'll hide if he can, holing up somewhere, and either heal or make life very difficult for whoever is around."

"And you can't blame Toby for that either," she declared, looking at him intently.

Bauer just let her stare, not sure what her problem was but still quite okay with her checking him out. He needed her to trust in him, when dealing with anything she had to offer in this case. "I'm all about being on the dog's side," he stated calmly.

"I'm sure glad to hear that. I knew Badger was handling War Dogs, and, once I'd scanned Toby and realized what I had, I reached out. I didn't expect it to go sideways like this. I did the surgery as soon as I could but had to stabilize Toby first, just to confirm he could even get through it. He was terribly dehydrated, and that leg was a disaster. And then, as soon as I get him through the damn surgery, some asshole comes in here and takes him." She shook her head. "Believe me. I've been kicking myself ever since. That dog is not out of the woods by any means, and, if we don't find Toby soon, he won't make it, and somebody is likely to get hurt."

"Sounds like you did all you could and more. Can I take a look at this video feed on my own?"

She stepped back and nodded. "Have at it. I've got to get back to work anyway." She stopped and added, "I don't know if you can even do anything, but please keep me informed, if you get anywhere on this."

"Will do. Hey, Mags. If I find him, he'll need treatment pretty quickly, right? So, are you available, like twenty-four/seven?"

"Of course," she declared. "It's my handiwork the dog is dealing with right now, and I'll need him back here, where I can ensure he is okay. Pain isn't the only issue. If Toby's out on his own, he's likely to be wet and dirty. Therefore, the odds of getting an infection started are pretty high. You call me the minute you find him."

Bauer nodded at that. "Wouldn't it be nice if it were that easy?"

With that, she gave him a look. "Make it as easy as that." Then she turned and walked back out again.

He knew what she meant, but it just wasn't that simple. Sometimes these things were not very easy at all. He quickly went through the security camera footage, and it wasn't much help. There was no sign of a camera on the parking lot or by the broken window. He walked back out to the receptionist and, finding her alone, asked her a couple questions. "So, the guy who came in asking about the War Dog, did you happen to see his vehicle?"

She shook her head. "No. Believe me. I wish I had."

He nodded. "That'll be a theme, I'm afraid, on this one. I was hoping for a lead so I would have something to track. I have a not-so-clear picture of his face, but that won't get me very far."

"He must have a place big enough to hold the dog."

"Which doesn't help much either, and, with an injured dog like that, depending on his condition at the time of the dognapping, it wouldn't have been that hard for this guy to take Toby away somewhere. Do you know whether the War Dog was awake, walking, or whatnot?"

She winced. "He should have been in a deep sleep for most of the night, but I don't know what kind of constitution this particular dog has." She looked back at Mags's inner office. "I don't know if you asked her, but she was the one who did the 2:00 a.m. check."

He frowned and looked back at her office. "She didn't mention that she'd seen the dog at that hour."

Now the receptionist's voice dropped. "I know she feels terribly guilty about the whole thing. It's just killing her to know that the dog is out there, suffering, and that she wasn't here to protect it."

"So, what is the system here, when you have patients that stay overnight?"

"Mags lives on the property, so she comes back and forth. Before she had the house here, she would stay here in the clinic."

He nodded. "I guess that's what I would have expected."

"And you would be right," Mags said, from the inner doorway. "I was here. I checked on Toby, and he was sedated. He was doing fine, yet I increased the pain meds ever-so-slightly, as I could see him shifting in his sleep. It's always better to try and keep the pain meds stable and steady, rather than trying to play catch up." She shook her head, "I definitely didn't expect to have the place broken into and the dog stolen right out from under my nose."

"Nobody is blaming you, Mags," Bauer said.

"It doesn't matter whether they are or not," she stated bluntly. "I blame myself." And, with that, she turned and walked away again.

"Whoa," he called out.

She stopped in the hallway, then spun around to look at him, one eyebrow raised.

"Did you see any vehicles around here?"

She frowned. "I walked across the property, directly here." She stared out a window thoughtfully, "I wouldn't have seen the front of the clinic and its parking lot from the house, so I guess the answer to that question is no," she replied reluctantly.

"And no cameras are anywhere along the parking lot, right?"

"No, but believe me, that will be changing now."

He nodded, knowing that changing it now wouldn't be enough to help the War Dog. With that little bit of information, several photos of Toby, with images of his injuries—so Bauer could confirm he had the right dog—Bauer headed back outside again. The window guys were long gone.

Although a few vehicles pulled in for the clinic's services, the area looked relatively untouched—except for the fact that a break-in always changed things, including the whole concept of safety and security. He didn't know if Mags realized it yet, but it would get a lot harder for her to be so blasé about it. He already could tell how twisted up she was about Toby's fate. He pulled out his phone and sent her a text message, asking if she could contact the other vet clinics.

Instead of responding by text, she phoned him. "Where are you?"

"I'm outside, checking the security options."

"Oh," she said, nonplussed.

"Why?"

"I thought you had already left."

"I'm still doing what I would consider due diligence before I leave," he explained. "It had just occurred to me that, if this dog needs help, and the guy finally decides to do something about it, he'll have to get another vet to look at Toby."

"Yeah, that's quite true," she agreed. "I did consider that, and I have an email half drafted. I'll get it finished up and sent out to everybody else in the area."

"Don't be shy about expanding the range here," Bauer suggested. "I wouldn't be at all surprised if this guy travels one hundred miles, if not more. He could just be on the road and traveling God-only-knows how far. I don't know what kind of network you have, but it's worth a shot to put it to good use."

"Quite a big one, actually. I belong to the vet association for New Mexico. And we have quite a collection of people here," she shared thoughtfully, "so you're right. I'll contact everybody and ask them to keep a look out. Let me know if you find anything, please."

He heard the note of desperation in her voice. "I will," he reassured her. "In the meantime, I'll check to see if we can access the traffic cameras and try to find a vehicle that would fit the time frame."

"Oh, that's a good idea," she noted. "I hadn't considered that."

"You did phone the cops though, right?"

She hesitated, then went on, sounding reluctant. "I did, but they weren't terribly happy with me."

"Why?"

"I guess they figured I should have stayed in the place overnight."

"What? But you were here on a regular schedule and had recently checked Toby. If you had thought staying was medically necessary, you would have slept here, right?"

"Sure, but Toby's vitals were stable, and everything was fine. However, knowing what I know now, it would have been better if I'd stayed here and—"

Bauer interrupted her immediately. "Don't even go there. If this guy was serious, and he wanted that dog, it wouldn't have mattered if you were here, and it could have gone really badly for you. As much as I hate to say it, this is better than having you injured in the process."

"I wondered about that," she muttered, "but it's pretty hard to reconcile the grief of the loss with a minor plus in all this."

"I get it," Bauer said. "Still, you need to stay strong, and no good comes from you feeling guilty. I'll let you know if anything turns up." And, with that, he ended the call.

MAGS WORKED HER way through the day, struggling with the sadness and the guilt. It had been over eight hours now. Toby was a hell of a dog, and she'd connected with him from the first moment he'd arrived. But then she always had a hard time not connecting to animals, particularly animals in need. She'd been working with Toby for a good week if not ten days now, hoping to save that leg before confirming it was best to remove it. She would have to check her records, but it seemed as if he'd always been here; yet she knew she would need to get him adopted by another family, which was when she had called Badger.

The break-in last night had been shocking, since it seemed it was planned, with Toby as the target. It was also surprising since she hadn't had any security problems at all, up until then. It bothered her, since it came on the heels of the one stranger yesterday, who'd come in asking about Toby. She'd been quite happy to talk about Toby with the man, including explaining about the whole adoption process. Obviously he didn't like the sounds of that, and, although Mags couldn't be sure he was the guilty party involved in the dognapping, it sure seemed likely.

But seeming *likely* also wasn't a conviction. Supposedly people were innocent until proven guilty, but, in her heart of hearts, she understood perfectly well that this guy, whoever he was, had wanted that dog and hadn't been too particular about how he went about getting Toby. The question was, why? When she'd pressed him for more details, he hadn't been forthcoming.

He had been dressed in camo gear, and she wondered whether he was one of those prepper types, who were very popular in the US now—or those who really personified the military but hadn't actually served. She knew there was probably a word for them but didn't quite know what it was. She also didn't understand that mentality. I mean, if you love the military, then go sign up. Of course not everybody was eligible. Not everybody passed the physicals. Plus there were all kinds of other reasons why some couldn't get in.

But Toby, as a War Dog, had done his time. Judging by his scars, Toby had worked damn hard, had trained, and had suffered badly while in service to the nation—not to mention whatever had happened that resulted in him being left near the clinic, badly injured and abandoned. Bauer and Badger probably never would figure out that part.

She just didn't want Toby to suffer anymore. This guy who dognapped Toby might know how to look after the dog, but he might not. And the fact that the dognapper had intentionally taken Toby away post-surgery was unforgiveable, considering that pain management and the potential for infection typically required close follow-up care.

As far as Mags was concerned, it was one thing to take an animal but quite another to cause it unnecessary hardship. And, in this case, the dognapper just didn't care.

That guy knew perfectly well the War Dog would need both time and care because Mags had spelled that out for him. If he was a prospective adopter, he must know all the responsibilities entailed with Toby. The guy also didn't appear prepared to put any kind of money into the War Dog's care or to help cover current costs. He sure didn't make any such offers.

She didn't know the criteria to adopt a military dog like Toby, but maybe it was something she should look into, just so she had a better idea how the system worked. But honestly, at the moment, she was still too overwrought over the poor missing dog to even contemplate what would need to happen for Toby to get adopted out of here safely. They had to find him first.

She wandered through the surgery area, where Toby had been recovering in an open crate. She frowned at the sight of the tubes and other items scattered about, then immediately picked up her phone and called Bauer. When he answered, sounding distracted, she said, "I don't know if there is funding for such a thing, but I just realized that the dognapper had ripped out the IV lines and everything else from Toby, so there could potentially be fingerprints or DNA left behind."

"*Interesting.* Let me check on that, and I'll get back to you."

When she looked up at a noise, Sarah walked in. "Problems?" Mags asked, as Sarah looked at the empty cage, and her bottom lip trembled. "I know," Mags said, with a nod. "I was just wondering if they could get fingerprints or anything off any of this."

Sarah frowned at her. "I didn't even think that was possible."

"Honestly I don't know that it is," Mags noted, with a shrug. "Not to mention the cost factor involved."

"Right. But if they could—"

"I just asked Bauer, and he'll check and get back to me." Her phone rang almost immediately.

"I'm on my way over to take fingerprints," Bauer announced.

"Can you do that?"

"I can."

He didn't elaborate, and she didn't ask. He had ended the call already. She pocketed her phone. "He's on his way back. Apparently he can take the fingerprints."

"That would be good. I suppose it still costs money to get it run though."

Mags grimaced, while nodding. "Just one more thing we're up against right now." She looked around and asked, "Did the security guys talk to you before they left?"

Sarah shook her head. "Just to say they would be back this afternoon though."

She shrugged. "Of course they will. Nothing is ever as simple as getting to the bottom of anything in one trip anymore. It takes multiple visits every time now, which I never understand."

"I think it was something about stock issues for the replacement window that they were looking into and to get you a price."

"As much as I don't want to pay for that, it's not something I have a lot of choice in. I'm sure my deductible is more than the replacement costs. Plus I can't have my windows busted out and expect anybody to trust me with their animals. And, right about now, I'm not sure I even trust myself."

"Hey, it's not your fault," Sarah stated.

"I know, and yet, at the same time, it is." Mags groaned. "What does our afternoon look like?"

"It's still relatively calm," Sarah noted. "You've got several more appointments, but it's lunchtime now."

Mags smiled. "That's a good thing because I do need some coffee." And, with that, she turned and walked toward the coffeepot. "I wish I had noticed something when I returned last night, but I came from the other side of the property, so no way to see what was happening on this side."

"But there's no sense in beating yourself up over it," Sarah told her boss and friend. "It's really not your fault."

She looked at her. "You know you can say that until you're blue in the face but ..."

"I know, and you aren't listening to me. I get it, and I'm sure, if it were me, I would probably feel the same way, but we must focus on what we *can* do something about."

Just then Bauer walked in the front door, looked at her, and asked, "Where is it?" She led the way to the back, where the cage was, then watched as he sprayed the items in question first, then carefully took several fingerprints.

She muttered, "I don't think I even want to know how you got that."

"Good," Bauer replied cheerfully. "We have all kinds of tricks, but it'll take some doing to get this run through our system."

"Yeah, and what will that be?"

"I'll let Badger know, and we'll see if he can come up with somebody who can do it quickly," Bauer explained.

"We did call the police," Mags added.

Bauer shrugged. "I know, and I might take this to them too, but I'm leaving it with Badger for now."

"Would the cops trust your prints?"

"Maybe, if this triggered something positive. In that case, they would probably come running themselves. The problem is, the dog was taken, and nobody really cares. The fact that your clinic had a break-in, where there's drugs, would usually get their attention. However, since no drugs were taken, the cops will stop and consider if it's worth spending their resources." He looked over at her. "No drugs were taken, right?"

She nodded. "Not as far as I can tell."

"So, that's one thing," Bauer said. "I mean, we should be grateful for that as least."

"Are you sure?" she asked. "I guess I would have felt better if the dognapper had at least taken the painkillers. That would have made Toby's life easier."

Bauer winced. "I know, and I'm sorry because obviously Toby is the priority here, but, for the cops, it's not. It's just not a priority at all. The reality for them is that they have other cases stacked up that they probably have a better chance of solving."

"Maybe, but this one is pretty-damn fresh."

"Did they say anything when they were here?"

She shook her head. "No, not really. They took the information and told me that they would keep an eye out for the War Dog, then left."

Bauer nodded. "Okay, I'll head back with this. I'll give it to Badger and see if they've got any way to get something out of it. Apparently they have a connection out of California who might help get it run—or possibly even get us hooked up here in town. I don't know. Between Badger and Kat, they seem to have a pretty long reach. ... It's a little bit different working with them."

"But you don't actually work for them, do you?" Mags asked.

"No, not technically," Bauer replied, "but I did agree to take on this missing War Dog case. I'm not sure that gives me any extra benefits though." And, with a casual look around, he added, "Okay, I'll head back and start looking at security footage from the nearby street cams and see if I can find a lead." And, with that, he disappeared again.

Mags wandered out to the main reception area and saw several vehicles pull in. "I guess that means it's officially the start of my afternoon schedule, *huh?*"

"Yeah, and your lunch break is officially over, not that you ate anything," Sarah noted, with a chuckle. "Now it's back to the grind."

Mags rolled her eyes at that and returned to her office, knowing that, as soon as the afternoon appointments started, she would have hours put in before she got a chance to take a breather. She could only hope that, by the time the day was done, they had some answers. Otherwise, that poor War Dog would just be suffering.

And, with that, Mags got to work.

CHAPTER 2

W HEN MAGS GOT up the next morning, she checked her phone for any calls or texts from Badger or Bauer. *Nothing.* Frowning, she sent off a message to both, asking for an update. Nearly instantly she got a response back from Bauer.

Nothing yet.

Hating that answer, she quickly went through the motions of getting ready for work. As she walked across the yard and now into the clinic, Sarah was already inside. "Why are you here so early?" Mags asked.

She shrugged. "I couldn't sleep."

"That's a hell of an answer," she muttered.

"Why are you here so early then?"

Mags looked at Sarah and asked, "How early is it?"

At that, Sarah laughed. "It's only 7:00 a.m."

Mags groaned. "Right, so we're both bad."

"Or we're both good," Sarah disagreed cheerfully. "At least this way you know that we both care."

"I get that. I really do, but *jeez.*" She looked at her assistant. "Please tell me that you have coffee made."

At that, Sarah lifted her cup and smiled.

"Dang." Mags moved quickly to the back room. "Kind of makes coming in worthwhile if the coffee's already made."

"Oh, you would've come in early anyway," Sarah noted.

"Yeah, especially right now," Mags agreed.

"Although we didn't have any patients in overnight, so you could have stayed in bed longer."

"Yeah, but, once I'm awake, I'm done."

"I know, but that also shows how you don't have a life."

"A life? You're kidding. I know I don't have a life." Mags laughed. "I have my own business, so that pretty well wipes out any hopes of a normal life."

"It doesn't have to be that way, though," Sarah protested.

"I don't know. Everybody I know who has their own business works twenty-four hours a day, and, if they aren't, they feel like they ought to be."

"Maybe so, but it's all about that work-life balance thing, you know?"

"When you figure out how I should go about that, let me know," Mags stated. "At the moment there just seems to be way more work and responsibilities than time for relaxing."

"You've got to be intentional about taking time off."

"I know, and that's why you've been asking for another assistant. I keep trying to find somebody, but, so far, we just haven't found the right person."

"I agree, and I don't want you to get just anybody," Sarah declared, with an eyeroll. "The part-time surgery help has been a great addition. Ultimately I would prefer to just handle the front myself, but then you'll need another tech. You can't do it all."

"I know, and I thought it wasn't too bad, until Lisa left. What's that been, two weeks now?"

"Four actually," Sarah replied, with a wry look.

Mags stopped and stared. "Damn." She scrubbed at her

face. "We need to get that job posting up again."

"I've had it up, and I've been going through the résumés," Sarah told her, "but I'm not seeing anything that sounds terribly encouraging to date."

"How is that even possible? Who would have thought getting decent help would be such a headache? I don't know. Maybe it's our job posting." Mags frowned. "Maybe it's just not getting out the right message."

"That's possible," Sarah admitted. "Maybe it doesn't have the right terminology for optimal searching or something. Everything on the internet is supposed to be easier these days, but I think it's getting more complicated."

"Let's take a look at it later today, just to confirm nothing unexpected is going on. We also need to get another tech in here. Let's see if we can bring in four or five people to come in for interviews."

With that, Mags turned and headed to her office and the paperwork, … the stack of never-ending paperwork. She had invoices that needed to be cross-checked, and the bookkeeper was looking for a bunch of information, probably the old invoices that Mags was slacking on from last month. Mags groaned, as she sat down but hadn't even started when her phone rang. "Hey, Bauer. Anything?"

"We've got a line on the vehicle," he replied. "I'll email you the photo that I found on the traffic cameras. It looks suspicious to me, and I'm wondering if you might have seen it before. Have a look and see if there's any chance it might be the guy who came in."

"But I wouldn't know," she reminded him. "I didn't see his vehicle."

"Just take a look," Bauer repeated and, with that, he disconnected.

Frowning, she opened up her email and waited for it to load, then quickly clicked on it. As she brought it up, she studied the vehicle. Something about it was familiar, but she couldn't place it. She called out to Sarah on the intercom.

Sarah walked into the back, took one look at what Mags was pointing to, and said, "Yeah, we've had that vehicle here before." Then she stopped, crossed her arms over her chest, and added, "At least I think so."

"That's the thing. 'At least I think so' and 'Yes, I did see this' are two very different things. I think so myself, but I can't remember where, how, or when, even if it was just another client bringing in a patient," she pointed out. "I don't know. Bauer is asking."

"Of course he is," Sarah said. "I'm kind of glad he's on the case."

"It should be the cops though."

"Maybe, but, in this case, I just don't think it would ever be a priority with the cops. I don't know if you've heard, but the police have been really busy. Apparently the crime rate has gone way up, and, although our problems do count, we aren't counted as much, when it comes to the pecking order."

"Of course not," Mags grumbled, "with no loss of life, plus it was an animal, not humans involved. Still, we can't have it pushed under the rug either. Speaking of which, I'll give the cops a call and remind them that we're here. I have to get the case number, no matter what."

"You do that," Sarah said, with a wry look. "Let me know if any good comes from it. Personally I think they've done all that they'll do."

"*Great*," Mags muttered, "I wonder if they even know about Bauer."

"I don't know, but you might not want to mention it," Sarah suggested, as she walked toward the door again.

"Why not?"

"Because you don't want to do anything to get that whole Titanium group into trouble," Sarah said. "Not necessarily in trouble, but there could be some stepping on toes. You know how everybody gets when they think somebody is not sharing information or is butting into their jurisdiction."

"No, I don't know how it goes."

"As the daughter of a cop, I suggest you take my word of advice and keep the two lines of investigation separate. If they need to come together, they will, but let them do it on their own. Check with the police, but don't tell them how you've got another organization working on it." With that, Sarah left and headed out to the main desk.

Mags got up, refilled her coffee cup, and walked back to her office again.

Sitting down, she called the detective, but there was no answer. She left a message, saying that she was looking for an update on the break-in at her clinic. She had no sooner hung up when her phone rang. She picked it up to find the police officer calling her. "Hey, I just now left you a message."

"Sorry about that. I don't have any update to give you. We don't have very much at all to go on right now," he said, his voice apologetic.

"And yet I need to get that War Dog back," she told him.

"We're on it. I just can't tell you much." She hesitated and, in time, he added, "Look. We're doing our best."

And, with that, she had to be satisfied. She wasn't, but nothing she could do about it. Yet, in the same spirit, she picked up the phone again and called Badger.

"Hey," Badger replied. "If you're looking for an update, we don't have one."

"Thanks, that's exactly what the cops just told me."

"No surprise there. They are absolutely swamped in town right now. I'm surprised you even got a call back."

"I wasn't sure if I should mention anything about you guys working on this or not."

"I would do that myself, once they got a detective assigned. If you can give me his name and number, I'll call him right now and let him know what we're doing. That way nobody will get any surprises. It tends to go better that way."

She quickly provided the information. "Thanks, I would appreciate it, so I don't feel like I need to hide it."

"Oh, you definitely don't need to hide it," Badger declared. "I work with local law enforcement quite a bit."

"Really?" she asked curiously.

"Yeah, I do."

"That's interesting," she muttered. "Anyway I really want to get something accomplished on this case today, but maybe that's asking for too much. Sarah and I told Bauer that we couldn't commit to seeing that vehicle before."

"That's okay. We already tracked it down. It was dumped on the roadside about one mile from there."

"Dumped? As in broken down?"

"We're not sure how to look at it at this point," Badger noted. "It's not stolen, which is one of the things that we had wondered, but did you think you'd seen it in the past?"

"I wondered, as did my receptionist. It looked awfully familiar, but we couldn't say where or when we'd seen it. We do get a lot of clients through here," she shared, with that note of apology in her voice. Even though she tried her hardest, that sense of apology always seemed to come out.

"No, I get that," Badger stated. "If you do remember or if anything triggers a thought, let me or Bauer know."

"So, now that you've run into a dead end with a truck, then what?"

"I didn't say it was a dead end," Badger corrected. "We'll run down the owner of the vehicle and have a talk with them, but I'll get Bauer to touch base with you in a little bit. I know he's out taking a look at the truck right now, trying to see if it could have been the one that transported the dog."

"Oh, so you mean it's literally just sitting on the side of the road?"

"Exactly." Badger laughed. "So, give Bauer a chance to check it out, and then he'll get back to you." And, with that, Badger rang off.

Mags sat here for a long moment, happy that at least somebody was doing something. It wasn't fair to judge the police because she knew that their caseloads were pretty rough. But having somebody just dedicated to helping her out, that was pretty huge in her book. Taking advantage of being in early, she turned her attention to her paperwork backlog, until her first patient of the day walked in.

Her day would be all about seeing patients and doing double duty, since she had no vet tech to help, not even her assistant Sarah, who was manning the front desk. By the time Mags ran through the first three patients, dropping the files on her desk to complete later, she saw a message Sarah had left by the phone on her desk. It was a simple one-line note that read *Call Bauer*. She quickly pulled out her phone and dialed him. "Hey, I'm in between clients right now. What have you got?"

"I went and checked the vehicle found by the road. It

does look like it's the one that transported the dog. There is blood in the back and some hair too."

"But no sign of the dog?" she asked anxiously.

"No, nothing yet, but the vehicle was broken down. So, either he went and got another vehicle, or somebody came and picked him up."

"That's not much help," she muttered, clearly frustrated.

"No, but that's not really what I'm calling about either."

"What then?"

"If Toby got away, do you think he would come back to you?"

"Not necessarily. He would be dealing with a lot of pain. He could be disoriented too. So it's hard to say whether he could find his way back to the clinic or not. Whether he would even want to, from his perspective, is the other question. Even if I was attached to him, that doesn't mean he was attached to me. Plus I'm the one who did this to him."

"Right."

"Hang on a minute. Are you thinking there's a chance Toby is loose?"

"There's a chance," Bauer noted cautiously. "I'm just not sure."

"What will it take to know for sure?" she asked, her voice hardening. "Come on, Bauer. Don't play games with me."

"I don't play games," he said gently, "but neither do I want to sit here and give you false hope, only to find out I'm wrong."

She stopped, pulling herself back at that comment. "Okay, that's fair. I'm sorry. I'm just wrecked over this."

"I get that," Bauer noted. "So the question at this point in time is whether the man who took Toby still has him or whether Toby has escaped."

"I vote for the dog escaping," she replied. "It would depend on what kind of shape Toby was in when they broke down, I suppose. In theory, Toby could have been quite unconscious, so I don't know." She raised her free hand in frustration. "Sorry, I know that is absolutely no help."

"Just have your phone close by, in case I need you," he said. "I don't know quite what to plan for, but let's just keep in close contact to ensure there's no delay in reaching you, just in case."

"If you need me for Toby, call me right away, please."

"I will," he declared. "Just know that I'm doing whatever I can."

"I know that," she said. "I'm just so frustrated because I know that Toby's suffering. Earlier I spoke to the cop who was here yesterday about the break-in, but he didn't have any update."

"No, the only way he'll find anything is if there are reports of the dog showing up or any rumors about a dog being for sale. But, given Toby's physical condition, that's not likely."

"Jeez, I would hope not," she replied in horror. "Why would somebody try to sell Toby at this point?"

"Because people are idiots, and, if there's a certain prestige in some circles about owning a War Dog, maybe that's what the dognapper's trying to cash in on. But I don't know that, so let's not even go there," he clarified, with a warning.

"Right, right." She pinched the bridge of her nose. "This is making me crazy."

He chuckled. "It's good that you care. … Just try to stay focused on the facts, not the potential theories and possibilities."

"Easy for you to say," she muttered.

"No, not all that easy, as it turns out," he murmured. "I'll pop in before the end of the day, regardless of how it goes."

"Bring me the dog. You know how badly I need Toby back."

"What happens when you get him back?"

"I'll fix him. As much as I can, at least. Then I wouldn't even dare leave him here. I would probably take him home, to my house."

"You're that attached?"

"Absolutely not. Sort of. Honestly, I was of two minds as to whether I could talk Badger into letting me keep Toby. But I want to make sure he's okay, before putting him back out there."

"I'm not sure that there would be much talking required, since Badger's job is to confirm these animals are well looked after," Bauer explained. "So, I can't imagine anyone would think you keeping him would be a problem."

"Maybe," she conceded. "For years I deliberately didn't take in strays because I know there's no end to it. Yet just something about Toby drew me in."

"That's good to hear. Maybe he will try to come back to you."

"I don't know. You have to remember that I'm also the one who just took off his leg."

"But, if he was in a lot of pain before, he may not hold it against you."

"It's hard to say," she replied, but she knew she didn't sound very convinced at the idea. "Anyway, my next patient is here, so I've got to run. Keep me posted."

"Talk to you in a bit," Bauer said, then was gone.

She got up and walked in to see the next patient, followed by the one after that and the next one after that. By the time midafternoon rolled around, she walked out to the reception area and noted the waiting room was empty. "Is that it for the day?" she asked Sarah.

"No. Mrs. Sampson just canceled," Sarah shared in exasperation. "Her dog was doing much better, so she decided not to come in, and Beth is running late, so I'm not sure when she'll be here. She did phone to say that she was on the way, but she was definitely running behind."

"In that case I'll grab another coffee." Mags headed back to get it. As she walked back out with a steaming cup in hand, Sarah looked at her and asked, "Did you phone Bauer?"

"Yeah, a couple hours ago. Did he call again?" she asked, pulling out her cell phone.

"No, not since the one call earlier."

Mags nodded. "I was hoping he would, though. I mean, when he had some information." Because now that she had the hope that Toby could be loose somewhere, she couldn't get that out of her mind.

Just then, Beth walked in with her small Corgi.

"Hey," Mags greeted them. "Come on back, and we'll take a look." And that was the last thought she had for Toby for another half hour. By the time Mags walked out to the front lobby again, two more clients were waiting, and it just continued for the rest of the afternoon. When she was done for the day, she put the rest of the files on the ever-growing pile on her desk and sat with a *thud* and dropped her head in her hands.

Almost immediately a man said, "Now that's a tired look." She lifted her head and stared, as Bauer smiled back at her. "Hey, sorry. I didn't want to sit out in the waiting room, so I convinced Sarah to let me in here."

"That's fine." Mags gave him a wave of her hand. "It doesn't much matter. I'm just tired."

"Tired and stressed."

She smiled. "It all goes together, doesn't it?" She saw several messages waiting for her too. She stared at him. "Give me a minute to go through these messages, will you?"

"Sure."

She quickly flipped through the stack. She winced at the quote from the window guys but wrote it down. There was a message from the insurance company and one from her sister and some junk in between. None of which was important enough to hold her attention, given the current situation. She sat back, then looked at him. "Did Sarah offer you coffee?"

"No, but that's fine. I've had plenty of that today."

Mags nodded. "Me too. I think I'm swimming in the damn stuff." She looked over at him, waiting for any word.

"I'm hesitating to confirm it, but am seriously wondering if Toby did escape."

She just stared at him, her mind racing. "I don't even know if that's a good thing or a bad thing at this point."

"Me either, but it keeps bringing me back to the fact that the dog was injured." He studied Mags's features for a long moment. "The question is, what would he do if he did escape? I spent a little bit of time searching the area earlier, and there was some blood, but it rained this morning, ... so I'll go back out this evening and see what I can confirm from my vehicle, just looking at the surrounding location where the vehicle broke down. I wanted to see if you had any opinion on whether Toby would come here and whether he was capable of walking that far."

"Theoretically, yes. Toby was in a lot of pain before I took off his leg, but it wouldn't surprise me to think that he could continue to function quite normally, if not even better, because the leg was gone."

"Would there be a lot of pain?"

"Absolutely, but not necessarily from the mechanics of walking."

"And cornered, would Toby be dangerous?"

"Dangerous as hell. I would hope he would come here, but I know that's a bit far-fetched. I mean, I kept him in a cage the whole time. Even though I was looking after him, and I would like to think he understood that I was helping him, that doesn't mean he did," she shared.

Bauer nodded and stood. "Good enough then. Thanks." And, with that, he turned and started toward the door.

She called out, "Wait."

He looked back at her. "What?"

She hesitated, then shrugged. "Keep me in the loop."

He smiled, his features softening. "Always. ... One of these days we could go have a coffee or something and just be normal, instead of always bonding over animals."

She laughed. "That's what we do though, isn't it? Bond over animals."

"Maybe." Then, with an awfully cheerful note, he added, "But one of these days we could bond over coffee." And, with that, he was gone.

Mags frowned at the doorway.

Sarah poked her head around the corner and asked, "Did he just ask you out for coffee?"

"I think that's what that was," she muttered. "I'm just not quite sure."

"If it was, take him up on it."

"Why would I do that?" Mags asked, frowning at her assistant.

"Because he's cute. I kinda like his crooked smile," Sarah said, with a laugh. "His short dark hair and your auburn hair, falling out of the braid all the time, are good contrasts. He's ripcord lean, and you are all lightness, yet you are both strong personalities. Plus he's deep, and you're a girl who needs deep."

"What are you talking about?"

At that, Sarah rolled her eyes. "You'll never connect with anybody superficial. It's got to be somebody with more heart than common sense in a way. Although, at first glance, he doesn't quite fit the part."

"You think? No, I wouldn't think so." Mags had to laugh. "He would probably be quite insulted at your take on it."

"I think it might take a lot to insult him. He's very confident, even with that leg of his."

"So what if he's got a prosthetic? A lot of Badger's men do. Including Badger and Kat both, for that matter."

"I know, right? Just to think about what those people went through is pretty amazing."

"That's another reason to not even have it be part of the equation."

"I get that," Sarah said. "So, now that you've talked yourself into exactly the same thing, make sure you talk yourself into accepting his offer."

"It was hardly an offer," Mags argued. "It was one of those casual, back-door, around-the-bend offers. *So, maybe sometime, when life calms down, we could go do something like that.* It was hardly a serious suggestion."

Sarah frowned at Mags, as if she were some dummy.

"Oh, it was serious all right. If you ask me, he was testing the waters. You know something, Mags? For a really smart woman, sometimes you can be a little dense." And, with that, Sarah disappeared.

IT HAD BEEN a long day, with lots of running around and checking in on various things. Bauer had finally talked to the owner of the truck. The elderly woman told him that she didn't even know it was missing. When Bauer asked her when she had last used it, she shrugged, thought it was the previous week maybe. Then when he explained where it was found, she just stared at him in shock. When he told her that he was having the vehicle towed back to her, she was very appreciative.

Earlier he'd gone back to the vehicle and had taken a good look. Figuring out what was wrong with it, he had called a tow truck and had arranged to get it back to its rightful owner, after talking to the cops. But because it wasn't reported as stolen, and there was no way to prove that it was even involved in at least the theft of the dog, the cops had been okay with Bauer taking it away, after forensics had secured it.

Bauer considered that shortsighted on their part, but, from the cops' perspective, it was a case of too much conjecture and not enough actual evidence. Then, with a couple sandwiches in his pockets, a thermos of coffee, a bottle of water, and a leash in his backpack, he headed out to where he'd found the vehicle and started walking slowly back toward the vet clinic.

He had absolutely no idea if the War Dog was even

loose. He wanted Toby to be, but that desire didn't give Bauer any factual evidence. He had traced a lot of tracks around the area, including in the grass and the fields around here. To him that just added credence to the fact that the dog might very well have taken off on his dognapper, but what would it take for a dog in that condition? Bauer didn't know. Mags had mentioned how the surgery site had been fully bound with surgical dressings, and, short of it getting banged up, it would hold through the dognapping event, without too much bleeding initially. However, if Toby were up and moving around, then the bleeding would likely start again.

And, with that thought, Bauer headed into the brush, wondering just how far Toby would have gone before any blood signs would show up. Bauer needed something concrete to support his theory and to prove he wasn't just blowing in the wind here. So far, he found absolutely nothing. He kept walking and checking the area, looking for any sign of a dog or a blood trail, but he kept seeing tracks of a man instead. That made Bauer pick up his pace, hoping that it wasn't the same guy who had stolen the truck, who had stolen Toby. The tracks appeared not to have been from today, but that didn't mean that this guy had or had not already found the War Dog. The rain had been light, not enough to wash away the tracks.

As Bauer moved quietly through the almost waist-high grass, it was hard to see anything, and that was both good and bad because, if Bauer couldn't see much, nobody else could either. He stopped to check the area, looking for signs within the high grass and then kept on going. He thought he saw something up ahead, but, as he watched, it was a coyote moving steadily through the area, its nose down.

At that, Bauer frowned. The time was running by, but Bauer kept moving, and he wanted to keep going as fast as possible in the direction of the vet clinic, yet he didn't dare take a chance of missing *any* sign. He hadn't gone too much farther when he caught sight of something that made his heart flutter. The grasses were flattened, and a trail ran up through them. Also a bit of blood was on the ground. He bent down, took a closer look, then realized that a rabbit had died at that same spot. Swearing, he got up and kept moving rapidly through the grass. If the dog were here, Bauer would find it; there just wasn't any guarantee Bauer would find Toby anytime soon—or before this other guy did.

As Bauer walked carefully but steadily forward, searching the whole area, he thought he heard another voice off to the side. He slipped behind several trees and listened. And, sure enough, another man was wandering around, calling out for a dog.

Bauer frowned at that and watched him carefully. No way to get close enough to take a picture, although Bauer could walk up and say something to the man. However, Bauer didn't want to alert him to his presence. He didn't know if this was the same guy who had stolen the War Dog or somebody completely different. Either way, it was very interesting that he was here in the same area, looking for a dog. That made two of them.

Highly suspicious.

Bauer kept ever-so-slightly behind the man, keeping an eye on the trails that Bauer was following, as the man called out again and again. It almost sounded like he cared. And that was possible too. So maybe this guy was over the moon about the dog and just really wanted to have him in his life. That still didn't justify stealing Toby, not when Toby was injured, plus taking him from the post-surgery care that Toby so badly needed. And it sure as hell didn't justify breaking into the vet clinic and terrorizing Mags.

She had done nothing but look after animals and had gone well beyond the norm in Toby's case. But that didn't mean this guy knew anything about it. He may have interpreted the adoption process she told him about as being something that he might never pass and had chosen to take another route that would ensure his success. Although stealing a War Dog, especially in the condition Toby was in, wouldn't have ensured anything, if you really thought about it.

Stealthily, in case this guy had a reason for going where he was, Bauer just stayed at a parallel pace, keeping his gaze wide and checking on his GPS to see how far away the stranger was.

Bauer was about one and a half miles from where the truck had been found, heading deeper into the brush, yet also cross-country to where the vet clinic was located. He still wasn't quite convinced that the dog would go back to Mags. However, animals were very good at understanding who was there to help and who wasn't. But surely the War Dog knew to stay away from this other guy. If he'd escaped once, hopefully he would know to keep out of this man's range. But what if Toby wasn't capable of moving anymore? What if the pain or the blood loss had been too much?

Frowning at that possibility, Bauer kept moving, picking up the pace, as the other man started to swear in frustration.

"Where are you? Dammit, I can't just spend all day out here looking for you."

Bauer wondered at that because, if they were after the same dog, that may be what it would take.

Finally the other guy raised both hands and yelled, "Fine, you win. Stay out here. I'll come back tomorrow, and you damn-well better be here."

He seemed angry now, not as concerned about the War Dog, as himself. Bauer frowned at that.

And then the guy trudged back toward the road.

This caught Bauer's attention, since he hadn't seen a vehicle parked anywhere close by.

Again taking note of the GPS location, Bauer followed behind the other man, but, instead of coming back to the road where Bauer had parked, this guy went down another shorter crossroad, which more or less looked like the access road to a farmer's field. But, sure enough, a small car was parked there. Bauer got close enough to get the make and model, then quickly took a picture of it and sent it to Badger. Unfortunately getting the license plate proved to be impossible because the vehicle had none.

He quickly added an update to his text to Badger, then headed back, following the trail where the man had walked, literally taking his footprints every step of the way back again to where the other man had been. Reorienting himself, Bauer stopped and waited. He needed something to pop up and to give him an idea of what to do.

Off in the distance, he heard the coyote and mumbled under his breath, "Smart enough, aren't you? You'll let that dog die and come down after it, won't you? How hungry are you?" Most of the time, coyotes wouldn't go after something big like Toby, but, if hungry and seeing an opportunity with the injured dog, anything was possible. It was a food source, and sometimes one had to eat the other in order to survive. It sucked.

Nature was a bit brutal when it came to things like that,

but, right now, Bauer needed to find Toby and to ensure he didn't become part of the food chain. Bauer kept walking steadily. As he got a little farther away from the road and any sign of that vehicle, he tried several whistles used with military dogs. No way to know just what Toby's personal trainer or handlers would have used for any kind of extra training. Everybody had one, even though they weren't supposed to, but, if Bauer could just hit on the right one, it's possible the dog would respond.

However, if the dog were unconscious and incapable of responding, then Bauer couldn't do anything to get Toby to raise his head, and, within this long grass, even that wouldn't be much help. But Bauer kept at it, walking carefully and getting closer to something, he just didn't know what.

When he watched another coyote streak by, he headed in the direction of the coyotes. He had always trusted animals more than people. Animals had instincts, and people might not like what their instincts were telling them when they watched animals, but animals could be trusted. They would take Bauer somewhere; he just didn't know where.

CHAPTER 3

B ACK HOME MAGS finished doing the dishes, picked up a cup of herb tea, and stepped out onto her deck. She surveyed the area all around her, studying the fields and the brush.

"I don't know where you are, Toby, but please, if you can get anywhere, come here. I'll help you, and I promise I won't put you back in that cage."

She knew that he had disliked the cage. What animal did? They were sitting ducks and couldn't move. A victim in so many ways, yet in terms of a vet clinic, there weren't a whole lot of other options. But now all she felt was guilt. She felt guilty that his time with her had been so difficult and only got worse when he was taken.

Unable to help herself, she tossed back the last of her tea, then put on her hiking boots, grabbed a vest to protect her from the light breeze taking over the countryside around her, and headed out in the direction where the broken-down truck had been found. She knew it was only a faint hope because, even at this point in time, no way that War Dog would be anywhere close to the same position he'd last been in. If he was smart, he would have tried some different directions.

Stepping out strong, she lifted her face to the wind, letting him smell her—if Toby was close enough for that to be possible. Surely he wouldn't run from her, would he? No way to know.

She could only trust in her firm belief that animals knew exactly who was on their side and who wasn't. Toby would have come toward her if he could have. It was also a beautiful evening for traipsing around the fields near her place. Perfect. She opened the back gate, walking toward the hills around her. That gave her a little bit more of a view, not that it would help if the dog were lying down in this long grass.

This time of the year was making a hell of a difference in terms of visibility. The grass should have been cut and baled weeks ago, but apparently the property owners were not so inclined. As far as she knew, nobody ever looked after it. It was more wild grasses than anything.

It was great for any of the wildlife around, if that was their diet, but not so much for somebody trying to find something hidden in the grass. She kept on walking and then started to call out for him. "Hey, Toby! You around here?" In the distance, she thought she heard something.

She stopped, tilted her head to the side, and then called again but heard nothing. Her heart sinking, she kept walking for another hour. She thought she heard something another time, but it just ended up being nothing. Finally she came around to the rise in the hill and sat down, where she surveyed all the land below her. It was a beautiful spot, though a bit of a walk to get here, but so worth it. It was absolutely stunning.

She stared, watching carefully, looking for any sign of movement, any sign of something moving around down below. And yet again found a whole lot of nothing. With her heart sinking, she stayed where she was for a good twenty more minutes, sending up a silent prayer, hoping that Toby was safe, wherever he was.

"Come back, Toby," she whispered, her arms wrapped around her chest. "Dear God, please come back."

And with that final thought to the wind, she got to her feet and slowly started to walk toward home again. She hadn't gone very far when, all of a sudden, she heard something, something like a bark, something sharp. She turned and spun, but she lost her footing and dropped. As she dropped, she thought she heard something else. She stayed where she was for a moment, wondering if she heard what she thought she had.

At that, she bolted to her feet and looked around in the tall grass. She couldn't see anything, so she raced back up a little bit of a hill, so that she could get a better perspective on the world down below, surveying what was going on down there. Then she pulled out her phone and quickly texted Bauer. **Where are you? I thought I heard a shot.**

You did. Stay still.

And then she realized there was a chance that Bauer had seen her. She didn't see him, even if he had, or was that just her wishful thinking? **I'm up on a hillside**, she wrote back, **a couple miles from the clinic**.

I know. You're okay. I saw you.

She swore at that. She hadn't been trying to hide, but it never occurred to her that she would have been so visible that it would have caused a problem. She could only hope there wasn't a problem, but absolutely no way to know. She waited and waited and waited. Finally her phone buzzed. She looked down to see a message from Bauer.

I'm coming your way. Stay put.

By now it was pitch-black, and she wouldn't have an easy time walking anywhere. She was angry that it was taking this long. Surely Bauer could have left whatever was going on and gotten here faster. Rather than waiting for him, she quickly phoned him. "What the hell is going on?" she demanded.

"I'm not sure," he replied, "but I don't want you roaming around out here in the dark, while somebody is shooting."

"Was somebody out here?"

"There was, but that guy left earlier. I didn't see anybody else arrive, so I'm not sure how many players we've got here right now."

"That's just bullshit," she muttered, then hesitated.

"Unless he came back."

"It's possible that if you saw me—"

"He may have gone home, then come back with his gun," Bauer suggested.

"Do you think whoever it was shot Toby?"

"No, I don't think so, but I thought I had a line on Toby, and now I've lost him. I want to get you home, so I can come back out here again."

"No way. If you think Toby is out here, I want to be out here with him."

Bauer hesitated. "Look. I'm coming up to your spot. I'm probably about ten minutes out, so stay where you are, and we'll talk about it then."

"Nothing to talk about," she snapped. "I want to find Toby." And, with that, she hung up. When her phone buzzed again, she ignored him. She stepped around, took another close look at what was going on around her, but couldn't see anything, and decided that maybe it was safe enough to keep walking on her own. She took a step and then another, when one more shot rang out. She dropped to the ground and realized that whoever was out there had no intention of letting her take another step in any direction. She was effectively pinned in place.

When her phone buzzed again, she looked down to see Bauer's text.

Are you okay?

She responded, **Yes, but whoever's out there doesn't want me to move.**

Yeah, remember that part I said about staying put? I'll be there in a minute.

She texted back. **No, he'll shoot you.**

At that, the phone rang. "Stay where you are and keep your head down," he snapped. "This guy won't shoot me, and I'll be there in a minute but don't fucking move. Stay in one place, damn it." And, with that, he hung up.

She sat here in place and waited with bated breath, her arms wrapped around her knees and her head dropped, listening hard. When she heard footsteps approaching, she felt a sense of relief breaking inside. At least that was Bauer now. As she went to stand up, it occurred to her that he hadn't called out, texted, or did anything to identify himself. And based on the shooting, the other guy knew exactly where she was located.

Who was to say whether this was Bauer, the shooter, or somebody else entirely? Someone was heading her direction, but how could she know for sure? Swearing under her breath, she sat here, frozen, hoping beyond hope that it was Bauer.

"There you are!"

When the laughing voice rang out beside her, she realized it was a stranger, and that wasn't good.

Knowing this would most likely be the shooter, she

didn't know what to do but stay in place. When he spoke again, she realized he wasn't exactly sure where she was.

"Nice trick trying to hide out here in the darkness."

He was counting on her to say something or to react to his voice, giving away her position. And, with that, she knew that she didn't dare move or speak.

This guy would know who she was and would take her out. Yet there must be a reason he'd fired those warning shots. He either wanted to see her, talk to her, or something else, but the bottom line was that it wouldn't go well for her. Just then she heard more rustling in the grass and the pulling back on a trigger.

"Speak up, you stupid bitch, and at least let me know you're here. The fact that you took off just pisses me off." At that, she froze because it didn't even sound like this guy knew she was here. How did that happen?

Then her heart sank. Maybe he was looking for Toby. Was that possible? Had she even told him if the dog was male or female? He was acting like Toby was female, which didn't give Mags any confidence in his ability to know the difference. But then a lot of people assumed dogs were female, but just as many assumed they were male. She didn't know, but he was making her crazy.

"Where are you?" he yelled. "Come on. Let me get you some help. I saw you go down hard."

At that, she frowned. Just then came another noise off to the side, and, all of a sudden, he started shooting. She gasped in shock, wanting to get up and run. But she also knew that would turn the gun her way for sure. With her hands clapped over her ears, she sat here, curled up, until the bullets finally stopped raining down all around her.

"*There*," called out the gunman, right beside her. "I

don't know who the hell you are and what the hell you're doing following me, but that'll stop you now," he said, with a laugh. "Jeez, who would have thought a dog would be such a pain in the ass."

Then she realized this really was about the War Dog. She didn't know how it all went together, but it was about Toby.

Just then came a crack of thunder overhead, and a storm that she hadn't even been aware of was building on the horizon, due to arrive at any moment. And the skies opened up, soaking them in a heavy rain. The gunman at her side started swearing, but his voice was muffled and getting fainter—as if he were running away.

She cheered him on with a whisper. "Run, asshole, run."

She didn't want to deal with him, certainly not in this situation, and she definitely didn't want him out here, hunting down Toby. And along with that came the thought that all those bullets could have been directed at Bauer, and that was the last thing she wanted to happen. Suddenly she was grabbed from behind, a hand clapped over her mouth.

"It's me. Stay quiet," Bauer whispered against her ear.

She shuddered, twisted against him, wrapped her arms tightly around him, and hung on for dear life. With a sense of relief, joy, and almost a feeling of homecoming, he closed his arms around her and held her tight.

"It's okay," he whispered. "He's almost gone."

And, with that, Mags just burrowed in deeper.

AS SOON AS Bauer couldn't hear any more sounds from the gunman, he leaned back a little bit, tilted her head up, and asked, "Are you okay? Did he get you at all?"

She shook her head. "No." Her hands went to him again. "Were you hit?" she gasped.

"No, but let's get back up into the trees." Then he moved her up the hill, but it was already slippery, and she struggled with her footing. By the time they got into the relative safety and dryness of the trees, he pointed downward to lights on a road below that were moving away.

"That's him, isn't it? That bastard. He was talking so oddly, and I really didn't quite understand if he knew I was here or not. I don't get it. Yet he did talk about a dog."

"I know. I heard some of it. I'm not sure what that was about. Is he confused or off his rocker or trying to make us confused? It could have been any of the above," he admitted. "The good news is that he's gone right now."

"Do you think he shot Toby?"

"I don't know," Bauer replied, looking at her in concern. "I did think that I may have had a line on Toby, but now I'm not so sure."

"Seriously?" She stared at him in delight.

"I can't guarantee it though, and now this weather will make it that much harder. Plus, with the bullets flying around Toby, if he was capable of moving, no telling where he is now."

"Maybe not though, he may have just hunkered down. He can't possibly have any extra energy at this point."

"Hard to say."

She nodded. "The rain may continue for much longer. Although sometimes we get these heavy downpours, and then they're gone in a flash."

"That's what I'm hoping for," he said.

"It's just too unbelievable though. Why on earth would

he shoot Toby?"

"I don't know, but then we also don't know what may have happened between the two of them already."

"But if he wanted him badly enough to steal him, why try to shoot him now?"

Bauer asked, "So did it sound like the same guy who came to the clinic, asking about the War Dog?"

She hesitated. "I, … I can't be sure. With me, he had tried to act the part, you know? Until he heard the details on adopting a War Dog, and he dropped his facade and just got angry. Out here, he was probably his usual self, not what he shows the public." Mags sighed. "I can't confirm it was him."

Bauer didn't respond. She groaned. "I hate this shit."

"Yeah, you and me both." After a few moments, he asked, "What are the chances I can get you to stay here? I have to go see if I'm correct." She stared up at him in the darkness, not responding. He repeated, "It would be better if you did. I don't want to overwhelm the dog if it's him, but believe me. I will definitely call you."

Finally she let out a breath. "Fine, but you stay in contact the whole way."

He smiled. "With that guy gone, we don't have to be so quiet. I just want to confirm that we have a good idea where the shooter is and what the War Dog is up to."

She watched anxiously as he stepped back and started to move out into the darkness. "I can't even see where you are," she said.

"I know, and that's okay too," he murmured. "I won't be far, and we can continue to talk." And he kept talking to her the whole way. He needed her to keep calm, but, at the same time, he had his GPS on to have a good idea of where they were. With any luck, he could get to the spot where he had been before and could make up some of that time they had lost with all the shooting and chaos. Then he would have a good place to start the search later.

"I'm still here," he told her.

He walked quietly and then brought out the flashlight that he had packed, using it to search through the area. It didn't help that now there was a good chance the dog may have bolted because of the storm, the lightning, the thunder, the rain, plus the bullets flying—or worse, he could have been hit. It was hard enough walking in the darkness, but the slippery footing just added to the problems.

Bauer started his whistles again, knowing that Mags could hear them as well and could keep track of where Bauer was. Then, hearing a rustling beside him, he stepped out to the left and waited.

Then he heard it again.

"Toby?" Bauer asked quietly. "Is that you, buddy?" Almost immediately he heard another noise. As he waited, he checked the area with a flashlight. There was an ever-so-quiet noise off to the side. This time it was more like an odd whine, so Bauer slowly headed in that direction.

He caught sight of the War Dog's dark fur. He carefully moved to the animal's side, his hand going to his neck.

"It's okay, Toby. It's okay," he murmured gently, his good hand rubbing the dog at the neck. But, when he pulled back his hand, and it came away with blood, he swore, as he held the flashlight up into the sky and called out to Mags.

"Can you come to me?" he cried out. "I think I found Toby."

CHAPTER 4

MAGS RACED OVER in record time, stumbling in the dark, trying to get to the flashlight beacon as quickly as possible. Her heart raced and her palms turned sweaty as she got closer. "Is he okay?" she cried out.

"Nope, he sure isn't," Bauer replied, "but I think he will be."

Mags heard the lightness in his voice, relief washing over her. As she skidded down the last bit of the hillside, Toby struggled ahead of her to get away.

"Oh my God," she whispered. "Toby, Toby, it's okay. Calm down." The dog, as if hearing her voice, dropped back down again. She reached out a hand, placed it on his neck, and whispered, "Oh my." She looked up at Bauer. "We need to get him into surgery quickly."

He nodded. "I agree with you there. Take my flashlight. You light the way and let me pick him up."

"No!" Then she stopped because there weren't too many choices.

He looked over at her. "There's really no option."

She sighed. "You're right. It would be too hard to get any kind of a carrier up here, wouldn't it?"

"It would just take too long, and Toby needs help as soon as we can get it for him," Bauer noted. "Just grab the flashlight and let's go." He bent down and, in one smooth movement, picked up the dog, who growled and snapped at him.

She placed a hand on Toby's neck. "It's okay, buddy. It's okay." But she knew he didn't understand and that he was in pain, yet at the same time she couldn't do anything for him, not until they got down to the clinic.

"I should have brought a muzzle," Bauer said.

"I just hope he doesn't bite you."

"He's growling at me, but it's not connecting, so I don't guess he's trying too hard," Bauer noted, taking no mind of the continued snapping and growling. "Come on. Let's just go."

She stood here, staring at them both, instead of moving out. Then she dropped the flashlight beam to the ground and slowly picked out the smoothest and easiest path to the clinic. It would be a long trip in bad conditions, but thankfully it was mostly downhill. Knowing it was best that they just keep going, no matter what, they both focused on the task at hand.

When they finally got to the building, she quickly raced ahead, unlocked the door, and turned off the alarm. She pulled the door wider, so Bauer could make it through without bumping Toby.

She saw the strain in his arms, but he was still moving smoothly, not showing any signs of distress. She raced ahead of him again and opened up the door into one of the big surgery rooms, motioning at a big steel table.

"Put Toby down there." She pointed, then moved over to the sink and turned on the lights. Immediately she shoved up her sleeves and started washing up.

He looked at her and asked, "I guess I should be prepared to help too, *huh*?"

"Yes, please, I definitely may need it."

And, with that, she moved over to the dog to get a look at him. He wasn't being terribly cooperative, but then she understood. As she quickly checked on him, she saw the IV port was still in place, even though the tubes had been ripped away when he had been taken. Normally she would consider that unsterile and start over, but, in this case, time was of the essence. She quickly flushed the area, then connected an IV and started dripping in fluids, knowing Toby was bound to be dehydrated.

As soon as she confirmed that was flowing well, she added painkillers to the drip. The sooner Toby got some pain relief, the sooner she could check him out and get started. Once he was knocked out, and she had him secured on the table, she looked back to see Bauer, standing there watching her.

"How bad is it?" he asked.

"I don't know yet," she replied in a clipped voice, "but hopefully we will very soon." With that, she set herself to the task and began her examination. She checked first for new wounds, but they appeared to be fairly minor, considering. "He was shot, but the bullet didn't do much damage. It cut through the thick of his neck on the back here," she noted, pulling one of the big lights down closer, so they both could get a better look. "This is likely to be a flesh wound, so hopefully I can clean it up and put in a few stitches. We'll get that one fixed up first," she stated, as she continued to check him over. "Now the amputation site is likely a different story," she muttered, swearing, as she looked at the damaged bandage.

She quickly stripped off all the dressing and assessed the wound. She heard Bauer suck in a breath beside her. "It's not that bad," she noted. "It just needs to be cleaned up and rebandaged. The stitches held through all that, which is a huge relief. Once stitches rip out on a site like that, we can't restitch it. I would have to cut off more flesh, debride the area, trying to get back to a place where we could pull the raw flesh together again and place stitches in healthy tissue. However, so far, this doesn't look too bad. He's got to be in terrible pain, and I'm not exactly sure how much of his state is a combination of pain, exhaustion, and dehydration versus other new injuries."

And, with that, she continued her exam. "Can you help me for a minute? I want to get some X-rays to be certain there's nothing new that I don't know about. If you can help me position him, then I'll have you step out. We'll have to do that a few times to get all the views I need." She quickly put on her safety gear, then, over the next few minutes, they took several X-rays.

As she stood in front of a screen checking them over, she nodded. "See this right here? Those two ribs are cracked, and, judging from the angle of the break, I'm wondering if Toby had been the victim of a good hard kick." Typing in some commands, another set of X-rays popped up beside the first. "See this? These are the ones I took before, and the ribs were fine."

"Jeez, why would somebody kick Toby, especially considering how hurt he already was?" Bauer asked.

"It could be anything. He must have been in terrible pain, so he may have growled or snapped at his dognapper. Who knows? Maybe Toby even bit the guy."

The dog was fully sedated now, so she checked his mouth to look for any clues. She found blood, but that could be from all kinds of things. She showed it to Bauer and suggested, "It's hard to say, but our dognapper might have taken a bite."

"I hope so. I hope it was a good one."

She smiled. "You and me both, yet I don't want him coming back because he thinks this dog needs a bullet."

"It happens," Bauer noted. "I'll go take a look outside, if you don't need me for a few minutes."

"Nope, I'm good for now," she said. "While I've got him sedated, I'll stitch up his neck, then scrub him up a bit and rebandage his leg. I need to start a clean IV port and get that switched over. Afterward I'll run some labs and do a full analysis of what I'm seeing here," she shared. "I'll be busy for a while, so you go do you."

And, with that confirmation, he took off.

She looked down at Toby, a gentle hand on the rough of his neck. "I'm so sorry, sweetheart. I don't know why the hell this guy thought he should break in here and take you, but we'll make sure it doesn't happen again."

She knew the best way to do that was to move the dog to her house. Somebody might break into the clinic again, particularly since the broken window had just been boarded up. She hadn't yet had the time to get security cameras installed or to even clean up everything after the last break-in. She knew she was taking a chance by bringing Toby to her place as well. Particularly if anybody thought that's what she might have done.

At the same time, she had a better security system up there. It had come with the house as part of the build when she'd set it up originally, and she hadn't done anything to change it. Finally she straightened up, did a last bit of cleaning up around his neck, gave him a shot of vitamins and antibiotics, then returned to the sinks to wash up. As she stripped off the gloves, she looked up to see Bauer standing at the doorway. "Anything?" she asked.

He shook his head. "No, not at the moment."

She nodded. "I'll stay here with him in the building tonight," she said. "He's had a pretty rough go of it, and I want to make sure I can keep his pain levels down because I can't have him waking up and thrashing around." She eyed Toby intently. "I'm hoping to keep him sedated for a little bit longer, but I have to monitor it carefully because he's just been through an awful lot. After that, I want to get him up to my house."

Bauer stared at her.

She shrugged. "I'll feel better if he's up there. We haven't got any more security cameras hooked up here. The damn window is just boarded up for now. After what we saw tonight, it doesn't seem like this guy is in any mind-set to walk away from what he's doing."

"No, I'm not sure he is either," Bauer agreed. He looked down at the dog. "But moving Toby surely won't be easy."

"No, it won't be easy at all. I do have cages up there," she noted, "and I've done it before with animals that I needed to keep a closer eye on."

"Isn't that why you're supposed to have a bed here?" he asked, with a note of humor.

"Yeah, it sure is," she replied, with a smile, "but it is more comfortable for me up there. Plus, since I still have to keep functioning on a day-to-day basis, anything that works for my comfort and the dogs is important."

"I won't argue that," Bauer replied, "but moving the dog while sedated ..."

She nodded. "I'll crate him right now, and if we need to, ... I'll put him into one that I can move." And, with

Bauer's help, she finally had the dog confined and resting quietly. She sighed as she looked down at Toby. "I'm so sorry, sweetie."

"It's not your fault. Remember that," Bauer muttered.

"It's not my fault, and yet it is," she declared, without looking up. "I just don't understand what's going on and why. I mean, this dog has been through a lot already. Who gives a crap if he's here getting treatment or not?"

"I know. I hear you."

"I'm a little more concerned about the fact that that man was armed and was out there tonight."

"You and me both," Bauer stated. "I'll need you to contact the cops in the morning."

She looked at her watch and grimaced. "You mean, *in an hour?*"

He stared at her, then looked down at his own watch and winced. "Wow. How did that happen?"

"Oh, you know. It certainly won't be the first time I've seen the sunrise from here."

He nodded. "I'll run and get coffee and some breakfast. Can I bring you something?"

Surprised, she stared at him. "That wouldn't be a bad idea at all. It'll be a very long day."

"It will. Don't suppose you can cancel any of it, can you?"

"Not really, but at least it's not a surgery day, so I'll take that as a good thing. I'm not sure how much trust I would put in my hands later today," she admitted, with a sigh.

"But it's still bound to be a long day. Can you get in any help?"

She frowned at that, while considering it. "I might be able to. I'm not sure. I'll have to make a few phone calls."

At that, he nodded. "While I'm gone, I want you to lock up all the doors and stay inside. When I get back, I'll phone you from the parking lot."

She followed him to the front door and locked up everything behind him. As he left, she muttered to herself, "Won't do much good. I'll have staff here in an hour." Dreading having to explain it all to Sarah, Mags just shook her head. But the good news was, she had Toby back, and that was worth everything.

With a smile on her face, she headed back to where he was sleeping. She grabbed a blanket they kept in the cupboard, then curled up on the floor, next to his cage. If she could get even one hour of sleep right now, that would be a huge help.

It wouldn't be nearly enough, but, hey, she would take whatever she could get. With that, she closed her eyes and fell fast asleep.

BAUER WAITED AT the coffee shop. He was picking up breakfast sandwiches, coffees, and some muffins. While he waited for his order to be filled, he texted Badger. Instead of texting back, Badger called.

"That was a good night's work," he noted.

"I'm just glad we got the War Dog back, and he's being treated right now. In addition to what he had going on before, he's got two cracked ribs and a bullet wound in his neck. Considering the ground he covered and the number of bullets that were fired last night, we probably did all right. The questions I have are, what brought on all this, and how do I stop this guy from coming back?"

"I hear you there. I'll give her a call a bit later and talk to her about it."

"Yeah, I'm not sure what kind of shape she's in right now. She seems to think she'll do a full day at the office."

"Of course she does," Badger replied. "I also know there'll be people at her clinic all day to see her, some with appointments, some not. Plus a few emergency phone calls as well. Since she's the only vet in town, she'll feel that she's needed. So, as long as anybody needs her, she'll show up for the job."

"I know, but she's also exhausted."

"And wouldn't it be nice if we weren't always in that condition," Badger noted. "Now, what is it you need from me?"

"There was a vehicle parked down at the road last night that I think our guy took off in, before he came back later. I sent you photos of it."

"Yeah, but they aren't clear enough for us to do anything with them. I would like to tell you otherwise, but, because of the lighting and the angle and the distance, it's tough to get much."

"Right, so can you at least help me confirm the make and model? Then we can be watching for it."

"I can do that," Badger replied.

"I don't know if it's possible to cross-reference to the owners. I'm just wondering if anybody in this local area might be the person responsible. I'm still trying to figure out his motivation obviously."

"That'll be the hardest thing," Badger noted, "since it could be anything."

"I know, but now that we have the dog, Mags wants to take Toby to her place, the house on the property, and look after him up there. Yet she'll be down at the clinic for most of the day, so I'm not sure if that's a good idea or not. I mean, obviously I think it's a really crappy idea, but she probably won't listen."

At that, Badger burst out laughing. "No, that is true. She's all about the animals. However, as long as she's there during the day, the dog should be safe there."

"Or we'll end up bringing the shooter into the vet clinic. It depends on what his problem is with the dog. I mean, if the goal was to kill Toby, why didn't he kill the War Dog in the clinic in the first place, instead of trying to take it? That would have been an awful lot less trouble."

"What do you think is the issue?" Badger asked curiously.

"The only thing I can think of is that the dog tried to attack the dognapper at some point, either when he was trying to kidnap him or sometime afterward, maybe when he escaped. So, in theory, he may have just decided that he should kill him because of it. Which is still pretty far-fetched."

"Not all that far-fetched," Badger replied thoughtfully. "Dogs have been shot for a lot less. But what other kind of motivations could there be?"

"I don't know. That's part of the reason why I would like to get a broader sweep on this. I'm not sure that vehicle will even tell us anything, and certainly nothing around here gives me any kind of information. But you know that I need to keep trying because, after seeing this guy out there in the dark last night, shooting things up, I don't think he'll give up."

"Unless he was concerned about the dog being dangerous and thought it should be put down before anybody out for a hike got themselves hurt or killed," Badger pointed out.

"That's true. I hadn't thought of that."

"See? That's the thing. We don't know what's going on in this guy's head. It could be a decent motive, though misguided perhaps, but that's not necessarily the way it will stay."

"No, you're right. Anyway, if you can come up with any information, that would be helpful. I'll also keep an eye on the clinic today, you know, like park myself in a corner and just see what walks through."

"Do you think he'll come back?"

"He might. He might very well come back looking for the dog still or looking to see what happened and who might have been out there last night. I don't know."

"Do you think he's unstable?"

"It's possible. ... With the shots ringing out and then him taking off, it's hard to say. The rain is why he stopped, but that's another interesting point."

"Why?"

"Because the rain wouldn't have stopped us," he noted. "Yet this guy was a little unpredictable, like the weather in a way. I'll also run out early and take a look in the daylight. I want to see what there is for tracks, and I'm hoping to figure out what kind of footwear he wore."

"Oh, that's interesting," Badger said. "Good idea."

"I need to just ... even though the tracks from last night are probably mostly washed away, I want to at least double-check that I'm not missing something."

"Anything you can do to mark off something as done in your head is obviously helpful," Badger confirmed. "We'll keep working on our end."

With that, Bauer disconnected and turned around to see

the waitress moving toward him with his order in a bag. Taking it from her, he smiled, then walked out to his vehicle. He stopped for a moment, sniffed the air, and realized that everything would dry out pretty fast, which was better for him. If he had to go out and track, at least then he would be able to walk without adding to the puzzle.

He headed back to the clinic, and, as he parked here, it was still quiet. It was early, so the parking lot was still empty. As soon as he had his coffee, he would take a look at the tracks. He pulled out his phone and quickly called Mags. When there was no answer, he frowned. He called again and then again. Swearing, he walked around the building, checking all the windows. He didn't want to break in if he didn't have to, but he would if that was necessary.

Knowing that the alarm was on, but knowing how to shut it off, he headed to the front door, quickly picked the lock, stepped inside and shut off the alarm. He frowned because that was way-the-hell too easy. And, with that in mind, he raced back in the dark to where he had last seen her, then stopped short in the doorway, a slow smile spreading over his face.

There was a reason she hadn't heard his calls. She was sound asleep in front of the dog, one hand in the cage, her fingers slipped through the wires, and the dog's muzzle atop them, sleeping. Bauer sighed a happy sigh and whispered, "That's a good thing, and one hell of a lot better than what I was afraid it might be."

On that note, not wanting to wake her, knowing she would be up soon enough, Bauer placed one of the coffees and two of the sandwiches off to the side, where she would find them when she woke up.

Taking his coffee, he reset the alarm and walked back

outside, then stopped for a minute to eat a couple sandwiches, tossing the wrappers in the garbage. He picked up his coffee and began to retrace their steps from the night before, back to where they'd found Toby. It was a perfect time to keep an eye on her at the clinic but still go see if anything was worth tracking up there.

He couldn't get past the idea that something else was going on here. Something that would make no sense until he got all the pieces together.

He just wasn't there yet, and he needed to be, ... before this got any uglier.

It didn't take long to retrace his steps back to where they'd found the War Dog. As expected, the tracks were a mess. Between the going back and forth with Mags, Bauer with and without the dog, and the rain, it made it that much harder to see anything. But he checked over the area, looking carefully for any sign, as he followed the tracks back down to where the gunman had parked his car.

Boot tracks.

The owner of the boots had skidded and had slid quite a bit down the hill, which was not unexpected, given the amount of rain that had fallen so fast. That would make it twice as hard to find anything useful. As Bauer got down to where the car had been parked, he studied the ground carefully. Definitely some tracks were here, so he took a couple photos, knowing it would only be circumstantial evidence and not something that would stand up in court, not when it came to actual forensics. The priority of the case might be elevated now, since it wasn't just about the dog any longer. Now Bauer and Mags had a shootout to report in the woods behind the vet clinic.

That didn't necessarily mean anybody at the police station would give a shit, but the shooting packed more weight than the theft of a dog, even a War Dog. Bauer always wondered how people could treat animals the way they did. It wasn't in his DNA to do such a thing. He absolutely loved them and felt the benefit of having them in the world was a huge boon. But too many people used their animals to take out their anger and frustration at whatever else was going on in the world, something Bauer just couldn't comprehend. And yet *irked at the world* didn't feel like that was the issue in this case.

Bauer didn't know why, but that was the sense he had. As he wandered back and forth, he headed down to the nearest intersection, but, of course, there were no cameras, nothing like that here. They were just far enough out of town that nobody gave a crap. Not surprising, with only so much money to go around, so it didn't make sense to put up cameras this far out. It would only be beneficial for people like Bauer, who needed to see something at a particular time and date.

As he made his way back toward the vet clinic, he noted a couple vehicles pulling up at the front door.

Bauer kept an eye out and realized that one of the compact cars belonged to the receptionist, Sarah. The other he wasn't so sure about but presumably was another staff member. And, if Mags needed anything, it was help in that office, especially today. He continued on this trek back down, keeping an eye on the vehicles, but nobody came back out again. Presumably, by this point in time, they'd woken up Mags. As he walked in the entrance, he saw Sarah sitting there at the front desk, staring out the window.

He studied her gaze for a long moment, just to confirm nothing was odd about it. When she turned and smiled at him, he realized it was more of a pensive look than anything.

"Good morning," she said.

He nodded a greeting. "Is Mags awake?"

Sarah nodded. "Yes, but not necessarily very bright and cheerful."

"No? I left her coffee and some breakfast before I headed out looking for tracks. I assume she filled you in."

"Yes, and just the thought of all this going on around here is enough to give me the heebie-jeebies," she replied. "Personally I would like to lock up and to go home for the day."

"Can you?"

"According to her, *No, we cannot,*" she stated, with a shrug. "*People depend on us being here.*" Then she smiled. "My feelings aside, she's right. People do need this. It's just that, some days, it would be nice to turn around and to walk away from the chaos. Like today."

"I get it," he agreed. "Hopefully today will be an easier day."

"It's a fairly minor schedule in some ways," she noted, "because we have a groomer here today. So a lot of the traffic will be for her."

He nodded at that. "Interesting that you offer that here."

"I think it was Mags's attempt to bring more people through the doors. We have the space, especially on specific days, so why not. And actually it really has paid off."

He nodded but didn't say a whole lot about that. "Do you mind if I walk back to see her?"

At that, she waved him back. "Go for it. I think she's been expecting you anyway. She saw you up in the hills, stepped outside for a bit, then came inside and went to her office."

He smiled, then headed back to her office. He knocked on the closed door and, when she called out, pushed it open. "Hey. May I come in?"

She smiled and motioned at him. "Sure. Did you see anything?" she asked, as soon as he had the door shut.

He shook his head. "Nothing definitive, no. I followed the tracks back down to where the car was, but, with all that rain and lots of slipping and sliding, not a whole lot in the way of tracks to photograph."

"Not that I expected it," she admitted, "but it would be nice if we could catch a break one of these times."

He grinned at her. "Personally I think we caught a huge break."

She looked up at him, realized what he meant, and smiled. "I know. Just having Toby back makes me feel so much better," she agreed.

"How is he doing?"

"Pretty rough," she said. "He looks terrible—and probably feels worse—but it's nothing that a few days' rest and some therapy won't fix."

"That's good to hear," Bauer noted. "It could have been so much worse."

"Especially after that asshole started shooting everywhere," she snapped, glaring out the window. "I still don't get why people do crap like that."

"Unfortunately we'll never solve those larger questions about humanity," he stated. "So, let's move on to the next thing we can do something about. How long before Toby can be moved? You still want to take him up to your house? What does your day look like?"

She stared at him, nonplussed. "Are you serious about staying here for the day?"

He nodded. "Yeah, I think there's a good chance the gunman will come back. I'm almost certain he'll return to look for the dog. He'll want to see if he got him last night, and, if not, he'll check down here to see whether the dog came in or somebody found him and brought him in. If the shooter's any kind of a tracker at all, he'll see right away that we brought the dog out of there last night, but I doubt that our shooter has those skills."

"Right," she muttered, "but either way you expect him to show up. *Great.* I was hoping he would just go away."

"Maybe he will, but I don't believe in fairy tales very often. Do you?"

She winced. "No. Believing in fairy tales? … Let's just say it never did me any good."

He smirked. "In that case," he stated, looking at her shrewdly, "let's presume that this guy *will* be back—at least to maybe ask questions even—so you'll need to talk with Sarah and warn her."

"Right. Maybe we should do that together. Do you mind?" Not waiting for his answer, she hopped to her feet and called Sarah to come back to her office.

As Sarah came in, her coffee cup in her hand, she asked, "What's up? *Ugh*, if you're about to tell me that more crap will happen, I'm more than happy to go home."

At that, Mags looked over at Bauer. "Do you think it's dangerous?"

He shook his head. "Do I think so? No," he replied. "This guy, if he does come here, will probably ask questions. I wanted to give you both that heads-up, so that you two would be prepared. Sarah, if you can be on the lookout for somebody asking questions and acting suspicious, maybe nudge him a little and be ready to deal with him carefully, plus let us know immediately."

"I'm always half suspicious anyway," Sarah declared. "But, if he's coming in with a gun, that's not my cup of tea."

"I wouldn't want it to be your cup of tea either," Mags declared. She hesitated, then looked at her assistant and asked, "What does our caseload look like for today?"

"The groomer will be seeing clients, so more people will be in and out. However, for us, the schedule is just steady," she replied. "Not terrible, just steady."

"Okay." Mags frowned. "I don't want to ask you to stay if you're uncomfortable. I can handle the front desk, if you want to go home and just skip out of this."

Sarah hesitated, looking a bit embarrassed. "You know I want to go, but I also don't want to leave you here alone."

"I'll stay," Bauer said. "It won't be obvious, but I'll be nearby the entire day, watching to see if this guy shows up."

At that, Sarah looked at the two of them with relief. "In that case, I'll stay. I was just worried that, with the two of us here alone, it could get ugly."

"It still might get ugly," Bauer noted. "I won't lie to you about that. It's definitely possible, but I wouldn't even have you be open for business if I thought it would be a danger to the public."

"That's what I was questioning," Mags muttered. "The last thing I want is anybody else getting hurt here."

"We don't know for sure that this guy will even come back," he reminded her. "We don't know what his motivation is or what he might have in mind in terms of a potential next step."

At that, Sarah nodded. "Fine, I'll stay. We'll keep the clinic open and get through the schedule. If it doesn't get busy with extra patients or emergencies, maybe we'll close a little early," she suggested, looking over at her boss.

Mags replied, "Why don't we just see how it goes?"

And that's how they left it. As Sarah took off again, Mags looked over at him. "You would tell me if you thought it was dangerous, wouldn't you?"

"Of course. We've been friends for quite a while. I would never put you in any more danger or not be straight with you."

"We have been friends, haven't we? I guess I hadn't thought of it that way. I've just been so caught up in getting this mess resolved. I've been kind of a jerk to you, if I think back a day or two. Not how someone would treat a friend," she admitted, shaking her head.

"Look. We were both just doing our jobs. Don't worry about it," Bauer told her, with a smile. "So, the plan for the day. You do you, and we'll keep the dog here for the workday. I would also like to spend some time with Toby and have him get to know me a little better, so I don't have to fight with him anymore," he shared. "Are you comfortable with me going in to sit and talk with him a bit?"

She stood. "Yes, that's a great idea. Anything that makes Toby more comfortable is bound to help him heal."

At that, she walked around her desk and headed for the hallway. He got to his feet and followed. She smiled as they headed down to the back. "I wish I had a way to put some sort of an alarm back here," she added. "Then I wouldn't have to worry about somebody messing with the dog, while I'm busy with clients."

"I can always just stay back here," Bauer suggested, and as he looked at the windows along the back wall. "Actually that's not a bad idea because I could keep an eye on the hills up there too."

"What would that do for you?" she asked curiously.

"I'm expecting this guy to go back up there to look and see if he can find the dog he shot at."

"Right, so he'll be checking to see if he managed to kill Toby." She shuddered just saying that.

As she led the way into the back of the vet clinic, Bauer turned to study the layout and the lack of security. "I guess there really is no security in place back here, for something like this, is there?"

"I'm not even sure what *this* is," she stated. "And honestly I don't know any vet clinic that has security in case of a gunman coming in through a window to steal or to kill a dog."

He smiled at that. "You're probably right, but that's not quite what I meant."

She laughed. "Be honest. That's exactly what you meant."

He shrugged. "Okay, fine, for a worst-case scenario. However, I really was just trying to figure out if this guy could get in the back door without anybody knowing?"

"Theoretically, no. We keep it all locked up but—"

"I picked the lock and came in and found you sleeping this morning. So these locks won't keep anybody out who knows how to pick a lock." As he kept walking, he realized that she had stopped. Turning slowly, he looked back at her.

"You did what?" she asked.

He nodded. "When I came back with the coffee and food, the door was still locked, and you weren't answering your phone, so I was worried. Remember how we left it? I was supposed to call you to let me in, when I got back with breakfast. When I got here, you didn't answer, so I picked the lock, turned off the alarm, and came in."

She just stared at him, and he watched as she swallowed several times.

"I'm sorry. You didn't know, did you?"

"No, I didn't know, and I had no idea it was that easy," she whispered, feeling short of breath.

"Yeah, it is that easy. That's one of the reasons we need to get your security beefed up. And not just for this situation but for business as usual."

She nodded. "I just hadn't considered that anybody could do that."

"It's not hard," he said, "particularly for someone who has been trained with my kind of skills."

"But what are the chances this shooter guy has that kind of skills?"

He frowned at her. "What we can't do is make an assumption that he doesn't," he suggested. "So let's go on the assumption that there is a good chance that he could."

She nodded slowly. "*Great.*" Then she turned and headed to the back of the clinic.

Bauer stepped into the area lined with cages, each one empty, except for the one cage at the back. There, looking out at them with a watchful gaze, was Toby.

At that, Mags bent down and smiled at him. "Hey, Toby. How are you doing?" When his tail wagged ever-so-slightly, she nodded. "So, in other words you're doing okay, but you've felt a lot better, right, buddy?" She slowly reached through the cage and stroked his muzzle, pushing toward her hand. She looked over at Bauer. "As you can tell, he's pretty friendly."

"He is? That's great." He bent down and held his fingers up against the cage and let Toby sniff them.

Toby sniffed and then licked.

"Oh, that's lovely," Mags muttered.

"I imagine he remembers me," Bauer noted. "So anything that helps him to remember me is a good thing right now."

She smiled. "Isn't that the truth," she muttered. "It really does my heart good to see him at least appreciate that you're one of the good guys."

"Now, if only he knew how to tell us who the bad guy was," Bauer said.

At that comment, she nodded. "It's never that simple though, is it?"

"No, it sure isn't," Bauer confirmed, with a gentle smile. "Now, you head off to work. I'm sure you'll be busy enough to keep your mind occupied. I'll just sit here and visit with Toby. You might want to let Sarah know where I am and maybe give her my number."

"Oh, good idea. Now, keep it low-key with Toby. I don't want him moving around just yet. Don't let him get excited. Remember, keep it low-key," she warned.

He shook his head. "I won't get him riled up. I promise."

And, with that, she turned and headed out to start her day.

CHAPTER 5

EVEN THOUGH MAGS was tired before her workday even began, she was constantly busy, and she couldn't cut back and close early. She met with a steady stream of scheduled visits, plus worked in a number of urgent-care appointments. If she knew an animal would just get worse by waiting, she couldn't put them off another day, appointment or not. By the time the end of the workday rolled around for the clinic, Sarah had left, and Mags sat at her desk, trying to get the rest of her case notes and documentation done for the day.

She needed to check up on Toby again, but, so far, it seemed he was doing just fine. She was grateful that no more serious damage had been done through his hardship over the last couple days. As she quickly tried to finish up her paperwork, she realized she hadn't seen or heard from Bauer in the last little bit.

She struggled with his presence. Yet it was good to see him and good to have him around. She felt a sense of security in having him here, but she also knew he couldn't stay here all the time. It was not the kind of work he did, and she certainly wasn't in any position to hire a bodyguard. This was an extenuating circumstance, one that she needed to bring up with him.

But, at the moment, she knew it would likely piss him

off if she mentioned anything. She didn't know him that well, but she'd met him off and on over the last many years. There was certainly nothing *not* to like. Just because she'd sworn off men, or at least long-term relationships, that didn't mean she had to not like men in general.

By the time she finished her last report, she stood and stretched, just as she heard a voice at her office door.

"Are you done?"

She looked over at Bauer and nodded. "Yeah, finally. I have a rule about completing my case notes each day. It's a disaster if I don't. But, man, for what was supposed to be a fairly slow day, it ended up being crazy busy. I think it's almost as if fate overhears you. The minute you say something about it being an easy day, the universe slams into you."

"Really? We should fix that," he teased, with a smile.

She nodded in agreement. "That would be great, although, from a business perspective, being busy is a good thing. So maybe we better leave it be. I will say, Toby is good motivation for me. I've plowed through getting all these case notes done, so I could go check on him."

"He's doing just fine," Bauer shared.

She nodded. "That's good. It's a huge help to see that he won't have any long-term damage from this." She looked over Bauer, as they walked to the back. "Presumably it was a quiet day for you."

He nodded. "Yep, no sign of the shooter. I went back out and took another look, but no sign of him there either."

"That's huge," she said. "What do you think about trying to move Toby now?"

He raised his eyebrows. "I wondered if you still wanted to."

"I do. I've got to get some sleep tonight. I could stay here, but I would really rather be at home. Plus, if the shooter comes back, I would rather he destroy the clinic in a temper fit than go after me in the dark."

"Exactly," Bauer agreed. "If you were planning on staying here, I would be staying here too." She stared at him in surprise. He shrugged. "I'll hardly leave you in the lurch now," he stated.

"Yet your job is the War Dog."

"Yep." Bauer gave her a big smile. "And it looks to me like maybe this War Dog has a defender already."

She smiled. "As much as I would love to keep Toby, if somebody has a prior claim or a better claim on him, that would be fine with me too," she shared hesitantly. "I am very busy, and, if a War Dog needs a ton of work, I'm not sure what I would do."

"You would survive," Bauer replied. "I can talk to Badger about it."

"Don't mention anything yet. I mean, I've done everything I could in terms of keeping him safe, but I failed miserably on one very big aspect."

He shook his head at that. "You need to stop thinking about it being a failure."

"Hard to do," she muttered. "It seems pretty obvious to me that it's a hell of a failure."

"Nope, not at all. You couldn't have known Toby would be dognapped. Nobody could have. You said yourself that the guy asking about the War Dog wasn't threatening. You also noted that he didn't seem pleased with the requirements to adopt Toby from the government. Who would have thought someone would just skip that *legal adoption* part and go straight to dognapping?" he argued. "So stop taking on all that guilt."

She smiled. "You're just trying to let me off the hook," she said in a teasing voice.

He flashed a bright grin at her. "Hey, you're my favorite vet."

She rolled her eyes at that. "I'm probably the only vet you know."

He laughed out loud. "I don't know about the only vet, but you're definitely the one I know the best," he clarified. "Here's the deal. I won't leave you or Toby without backup, not until we get to the bottom of whatever the hell is going on here."

She nodded. "I appreciate that, ... and I know it's not part of your mandate here."

"I don't really have a mandate, so that means I get to do whatever I want." He shrugged. "Helping out Badger is really not a normal job in any way, shape, or form, so a lot of good things come with a deal like that."

"Sounds good to me," she replied, "as long as it won't piss off Badger." When Bauer frowned, she explained further. "Hey, I really like the pair of them. I know they've recommended my services to a lot of people. I don't want to do anything to make them regret it."

"I can't see that happening," Bauer noted, "but I get that it's still always business in the end, right?"

She nodded. "It is, even when you think it isn't." She eyed him intently.

"This is what you want to do with your life?" he asked, with a big grin.

"It's the only thing I've ever wanted to do with my life," she declared. "I talked to Kat about that once because I asked how she ended up in the field she's in. She told me that the only thing she ever wanted to do was to help people like her. And, you know, you've got to admire that."

"Absolutely," he agreed. "And yet you put yourself in a different boat."

She frowned at him, then shrugged. "I don't know about that, but this *is* what I wanted to do. I followed my heart, and here I am. Now, is it a good deal or the best deal for me? Maybe not. Sometimes, as with this dognapping mess," she pointed out, "it seems like a train wreck. However, most of the time it's a great deal for me because I get to do what I love."

With that, she crouched in front of Toby, whose tail started to wag. "How are you doing, boy?" She opened the cage, and Toby painfully got up. She winced but asked Toby, "Should we try to get you outside for a little bit of a walk and some fresh air?" As he stepped from the pen, he sniffed the air, then looked over at Bauer—as if to say, *You coming?*

He chuckled. "It's good to see him up and around."

"They do much better if they can walk around a bit. Anytime they can't, it's a whole different story about the state of their health and their future healing. They can lose interest and sometimes just give up, all because they can't move around," she murmured.

"Do you deal with large animals here?"

"I can," she clarified, "but there isn't very much of a market for it here. Not that many horses and cows in this area. I do have a client who has goats and another one with llamas though," she added, with a bright smile.

"I'm sure that's a fun thing."

"The animals are incredibly smart, so it can be fun," she replied, with a laugh. "But just when you think you understand them, they pull something over on you. Then I realize I have a surprising amount left to be learned."

"I don't think you ever understand quite all of it with animals like that," he added, nodding. "I've had no exposure to llamas at all, but goats definitely."

She chuckled. "They're fun, but you've got to be prepared for the fact that they get into everything."

"I'm also quite surprised, given all the land here, that you don't have a huge rescue operation."

"It's been something I've thought about," she murmured. "But, as you know, it's just me here. Maybe if I had a partner or could hire more staff, then who knows. Without some help, I could get myself into a lot of trouble that way."

He laughed. "Now *that* I can understand. I think I would find it very difficult to not keep every animal in need that crossed my path."

"Exactly. So far, I've done pretty well, and that's why I've kept my house clear, but Toby? ... Well, something about Toby hit my heart in a big way. I would love to keep him," she murmured.

Bauer nodded and didn't say anything else.

She led the way out the back door, then stopped and asked Bauer, "Do you think it's safe?"

He shrugged. "We won't know unless we try. I've already looked out several times, and I've been up there, but there's been no sign of anyone. So, if a sharpshooter is out there, I won't know anyway." She winced. Looking at her, he smiled and suggested, "Let me go first." He stepped outside, took a look around, then opened the door up wide. "With any luck, it's all clear."

She snorted at that. "Not sure I like your way of expressing that."

He smiled. "You know though, it would be an interesting thing if this guy were still around and still trying to get at Toby. We would really have to question the whole motivation behind it."

"Hell," she snapped, "I've been questioning that since the beginning. It doesn't make any sense to me, even when the guy first questioned me about the dog. I was quite happy to talk to him at the time because I was thinking Toby could be adopted. It also made me sad, but I knew it might be the best thing for Toby. Instead things went downhill from there."

"I just wonder how he heard about the dog in the first place, and I don't understand the motivation to get him. That is what we still have to find out."

She gently moved Toby out into the fenced yard and walked him around. He hobbled, not quite used to the missing leg, yet, because the leg had been so badly damaged before, he hadn't been using it back then either. Now with the leg gone, the whole joint felt and moved differently. With that weight gone, his balance was different as well. She watched his movements carefully.

"I'm not a vet," Bauer began, from his position beside her, "but it looks to me like Toby's handling things pretty well."

"He is. Antibiotics, plus medications for pain and inflammation, will help him pick up the pace a bit. Still, he hasn't had a chance to get adjusted to the amputation yet either. However, once he gets his balance adjusted, he'll do fine," she declared, with a smile.

"Now back to the question from earlier. What do you want to do with him overnight?"

"I want to take him home," she stated.

Bauer nodded. "Okay, that's what we'll do. I would prefer to do it in such a way that anybody watching us won't know."

She froze at that. "Do you really think he's watching us?"

"I don't know," he admitted. "What I don't want to do is find out the hard way."

"Okay, so what do you suggest we do?" she asked.

"I suggest we take him up in my truck or your car."

"I can do that. Does Toby have to stay in the crate?" she asked.

"He's moving around fairly well, but it would be easier during the night if he were in the crate. We could bring it separately."

"We can do that," she compromised.

While she was out walking Toby around the backyard, Bauer quickly loaded up the crate into the back of his truck. The building blocked any view of the parking lot from the hills nearby. So that was good. As soon as that was done, he rejoined Mags. "Why don't we take the dog inside through the back door and make it look like you're putting him away for the night. Then come outside with him through the front door, and we'll load him up in your car."

And that's what they did. She followed Toby's lead, but he looked to be handling the transfer pretty well. When they got to the vehicle, she looked over at Bauer. "I'm not sure Toby can jump."

"He doesn't have to." With an easy movement, Bauer bent down, scooped up the dog, and placed him in the back seat. "There you go, buddy." This time the dog didn't do anything but give them a tail wag and a small yelp.

"Toby didn't object to that," she said, with a laugh.

"Nope, no reason for him to. I just sprung him free." Bauer chuckled. "He knows I'm on his side." And, with her driving her vehicle, Toby lying on her back seat, and Bauer driving his pickup, with the crate hidden by a tarp in his bed, he quickly followed her up to her house. There, he repeated the process, and, with Toby on a leash, he walked him around the side of the house and then inside.

"Of course, when I take him out later, anybody will know that he's here," Mags noted.

"Maybe, but, since he's been out now for a bit, we can wait until dark, hopefully."

"That's true," she agreed. "I'm happy to give it a try."

"Good. I'll be staying close by." He raised his forefinger before she could disagree with him. "Yeah, so don't even think about arguing."

She frowned and then shrugged. "I don't even know what to say to that. ... I guess *thank you* would be most appropriate, but it feels odd to know that I need this kind of protection and that you're providing it."

"It doesn't need to feel odd. It's just me. I'm no stranger to you, so that makes it easier. The thing is, right now, this is the best answer. So let's just keep it that way."

She smiled. "I'm not arguing. Believe me. I'm more than happy to keep us all safe. It's just, you know, ... it's an odd scenario."

"On a happier note, I brought stuff for dinner. So, as long as you have a way to cook steaks, we're all set." Then he headed through the front door that she'd opened.

She followed quickly. "You brought steaks? When did you do that?"

"Earlier, when I got breakfast, I planned for dinner too. Stuck the groceries in your work fridge. Yep. So, I'm inviting myself for dinner."

She laughed. "I can hardly argue with a houseguest who cooks too."

"I'm a great cook," he shared, tossing her a grin. "So, come on. Let's get Toby settled, and then you can relax."

As soon as she had Toby inside, with food and water available to him, she turned to Bauer and asked, "How do you know I'm not relaxed?"

"Because you've been tense all day," he replied. "You need to unwind a bit too."

"That's easier said than done," she stated ruefully. "I mean, how do you even begin to do that?"

"Sometimes it works, and sometimes it doesn't," he conceded, "but you've got to keep trying."

She shrugged. "I've got a bottle of wine. I was thinking about opening that."

"Perfect"—he gave her a grin—"as long as you'll share."

She asked, "Are you sharing the steaks?"

He flashed her a bright smile. "Absolutely."

BAUER WANTED MAGS to relax and to chill with a glass of wine and with being at home again. Yet it wasn't working. "It's really hard for you to unwind, isn't it?" he murmured.

"Today, it is, yes," she admitted. "I mean, it's an unusual situation for me."

"No, I get it," he said. "I'm glad I brought the steaks."

"I am too." She laughed. "I'm not sure what I would have had to eat otherwise."

"You do look after yourself, right?" he asked, studying her.

"Sure, but I look after the animals first, and then, with whatever energy is left, I use it to look after me."

"Sounds like maybe you need somebody to help look after you," he suggested, couched with a smile.

"Yeah, well, that's not likely to happen," she shared. When he turned to face her, she shrugged. "It's just some unpleasant history."

"Yeah, I've got some of that myself," he noted, "but, you know, it's *history*. It's not supposed to keep bothering us."

"Does that work for you?" she asked in a wry tone.

He thought about it before replying. "I think what has worked best for me was just the passage of time. And knowing how that stage of my life was over and that I was moving toward something new and different."

"*New and different* would be great," she uttered, with a sigh. "I'm not sure that happens very easily."

"No, not easily," he agreed, "but that doesn't mean it's not worth doing."

"Agreed," she murmured.

After a few moments, he asked, "Do you feel like telling me what that history is?"

"You first," she said abruptly, as she got up and grabbed the wine, topping off her glass and then his.

"Need wine to fortify?" he teased. "Tell me. Is it that bad?"

"No, it's just the usual sad tale. I found out two days before my wedding that my husband-to-be was sleeping with my best friend." Mags shook her head. "He told me that I was too busy looking after animals to have any time for him."

"Wow, that's shitty."

"I suppose that was his excuse, you know?"

"Why didn't he call off the wedding instead?"

"Yeah, I'm not sure. I think he was still looking at his options, trying to figure out what was the best answer, and then, when I caught them, he probably felt a huge sense of relief. I even wondered if he had deliberately set it up so I would find out, which just made me feel even worse."

"Of course it did. What a gutless bastard," Bauer stated, shaking his head.

"Gutless is right. They broke up not long afterward. My best friend eventually apologized, for whatever good that did. I could never trust her anymore. She did say that he was complaining to her how she should be more like me. Can you believe that? In my opinion, he would never be happy, no matter who he was with. Don't know who he's cheating on now, but it's that poor woman's problem."

"Gotta love people sometimes," Bauer quipped.

"No, you don't. I love animals instead. People suck."

At that, he burst out laughing.

"Okay, so what's your story?" she challenged him.

"While I was overseas on a mission, my wife decided that my best friend was a better deal. So, I got the proverbial 'Dear John' letter, and she divorced me and married my best friend, all during one tour abroad."

"Wow." She stared at him in surprise. "Did you ever wonder if your best friend was only your best friend because he wanted to get close to that other person in your life?" she asked.

"I don't know," Bauer admitted. "I didn't see any indication of that beforehand. However, he didn't go into the service, so, from her perspective, that was perfect because he would be around to look after her."

"And is that what she wanted? Looking after?"

He nodded. "I hadn't really thought about it, but that's exactly what she was looking for."

"And mine was looking for somebody to stay home and to look after him, I think. It's odd that we both got screwed over on the same thing."

"Maybe, but, on the other hand, it's good in a way because we both understand where we're coming from."

She shifted on her chair. "Did it affect how you related with others afterward?"

"Sure." He chuckled, but there was a sadness to it. "I never pursued another long-term relationship—or even a commitment. And, as you know too, it takes a lot for me to trust someone."

"Ditto."

"But, over time, it gets better." Not that he'd given it much thought. Until now.

"I guess," she muttered, staring off into the distance.

He sighed. "Anyway, I just thought, if we cleared the air on all that, maybe somewhere down the road you wouldn't be averse to going out for dinner sometime. No pressure though."

She raised her eyebrows, then smiled. "I would really like that."

He grinned. "Good. Great."

She had to agree. Long after that, they were ready to turn in, after a night of no sleep the previous evening. As they took the dog out one last time, she asked, "Are you staying here then?"

"I am," he declared. "Didn't I make that clear earlier?"

"You said you would be close. I just wasn't sure. I'm giving you another chance for an out."

"I don't want *an out*," he stated. "I want this bastard

caught."

"Yeah, me too." On that note, she headed off to bed, after giving Bauer everything he needed for the night.

Bauer laid down on the couch in her spare bedroom. Toby had wandered in, checking things out, then had moved on, probably heading for her bedroom. Bauer just smiled. "It's okay, buddy. Pick a spot, wherever you'll be comfortable." Bauer had been initially surprised that Mags wasn't crating Toby, when he was obviously still injured, but Bauer also understood Toby's need to move around and to check things out. So Bauer was good with it.

What they all needed was sleep, but Bauer also needed to confirm that this asshole gunman didn't come knocking. If he did, Bauer had to be awake enough to respond because this guy would come loaded for bear. No matter what, the last thing Bauer wanted at this point was to see either Toby or Mags injured or killed because somebody else had decided they needed to die.

Things like that just pissed off Bauer. As he lay here, thinking about everything that had happened over these last few days and what Mags had shared about her past, Bauer realized the advice he had given her earlier tonight was true. The thing that had worked for him the best with his wife's betrayal had been just the passage of enough time. Sure, he was a little more bitter and a lot more aware now. He was a whole lot less innocent about relationships and people in general, but he'd learned from his divorce.

Moving on was the trick, and that was something he wasn't sure Mags had done or was even ready to do yet. And, once that thought had entered Bauer's mind, all he could think about was how to help her get past it, so there might be something the two of them could take a look at in the future.

Badger would think it was hysterical, so thankfully he didn't know. Badger also didn't know what was good for Bauer. It was best if it stayed that way. Badger and Kat were far too intuitive already. In fact, if they already knew that Bauer liked Mags to begin with, chances were, that was exactly why he got this particular War Dog job. Those two could be devious in their matchmaking.

Bauer thought about sending Badger a text, asking him, then Bauer realized that just asking the question would then open the door for a lot more in the way of questions. Thus Bauer would be way better off just keeping his mouth shut. And, with that, he rolled over and went to sleep.

When he woke up a few hours later, he lay here and re-oriented himself as to where he was sleeping. Recognition didn't take long to kick in, and he knew where he was and why. Yet something had woken him. He got up slowly, wandered over to the window and stared out into the darkness around him.

It's possible that it was just his internal clock saying it was time to get up and walk around and to take a look. He realized he couldn't see anything from this window of the house, with the clinic on the other side. He headed to the main living room and looked out there. When a voice spoke beside him, he turned to see Mags, sitting on the couch. The moon half hidden by clouds shone gently into the room. "What's the matter? Couldn't you sleep?"

She shrugged. "I slept, but then I woke up suddenly. I couldn't see any reason for it, but I found it hard to go back to sleep."

He looked around in the darkness to see Toby lying at her feet. "How is Toby?"

"Honestly that's the first thing I checked. He appears to be fine, but he's a little unsettled himself."

Bauer watched, as Toby got up and paced around, then the War Dog looked over at him. "I think he has to go out."

"I figured he did," she confirmed, "but I was trying to decide whether it was safe or not."

"I'll take him," Bauer offered.

"How about we both take him," she countered, with a smile. "Then I won't feel so bad going out without your permission." Such a note of laughter filled her voice that he realized she was joking but, at the same time, was not.

"Thank you for not going out alone," he stated. "I get that Toby has needs, plus, given all he's been through, his internal clock is likely out of whack too."

"Exactly." Mags nodded. "He's upset about something, and I don't know what. However, given what he's just been through, I didn't necessarily want to go out, just in case an unpleasant visitor was out there, waiting for us."

"Give me a minute," Bauer said. He quickly raced back upstairs, and what she didn't know was that he picked up his service weapon. He slipped the handgun into his shoulder holster, put on his sweater over it, and hurried back down-stairs.

She looked at him a surprise. "It's not cold out."

"I wasn't sure how long we'd be out there."

She hesitated, then frowned. "Did you just pick up a weapon?"

"I did," he replied cheerfully. "Any problem with that?"

"I don't know. ... I guess not if we need it."

"Do you want to be up against this guy and *not* have a weapon?" he asked her quietly.

"I'd rather not be dealing with weapons at all and don't

necessarily like them around me, but having that guy shooting the way he did out there last night changed my position a bit. If there's a need for it, I won't be a fool about it."

"Good, so let's go out and take the dog for a short walk, and hopefully we won't see anybody." She led the way, but when she went to open the door, he cut her off. "Let me." Then he stepped out into the night. The moon was high, but the clouds gave it a half-light, half-dark scenario.

"It's beautiful out here," she whispered, as she stepped out behind him.

He nodded. "Two o'clock in the morning is the witching hour to me. Most things are asleep, and those that aren't should be."

She looked over at him sharply, but he didn't elaborate. There was no need to. She knew the scenario out here just as well as he did. She muttered, "I still don't understand what the guy's motivation would be."

"That's the key, and, once we know that, we might have a chance of stopping this. However, until we understand his reasons for doing what he's doing, it won't be so easy."

"I want to think that he's just crazy, you know, because, if he's not crazy, and he's doing this very specifically, that's a very twisted mind-set."

"I know, but it's never quite so simple. *Crazy* isn't just about being crazy because they could be high on drugs, or they could be dealing with all kinds of stress or trauma, and this might have triggered something. Maybe what he's seeing is not what's there."

She looked at him sharply. "You mean, like PTSD?"

"I don't even know that I mean anything specifically. I'm just saying that what triggers people into action can be quite different from what we expect their triggers to be."

"See? I never really spent much time studying humans," she admitted. "It was enough to keep studying animals. Animals made sense to me. People? Not so much."

He chuckled, as he walked alongside her. She shivered in the darkness, and he pulled off his sweater and wrapped it around her shoulders.

She caught sight of the weapon in his holster and sighed. "You wear that as if you're used to it."

"I am," he declared, "and, yes, I do have a license for it."

"That's nice. I've often wondered about whether I should get one, but it's just not something I'm comfortable with."

"Not being comfortable with a gun doesn't mean that you shouldn't be. Sometimes just even learning how to use them and being good with it is all you need. But, most important, don't even mess with having a weapon if you're not prepared to use it."

"And again I don't really want to be in that position, so I haven't gone that way," she noted, with a stilted laugh. "My father used them all the time."

"Did that bother you?"

"No, it didn't, but I was of an age where nothing much bothered me," she noted. "As I got older, it bothered me a lot more, which my father didn't understand because, if I would be a vet, I had to learn to live with death. I remember a friend of mine, well, two friends. One was going into medicine, and the other was going into vet school. They told me that the only difference was that one learned to save a life and the other learned to take a life," she shared. "I found that extremely hard to get accustomed to, but it is right in a way because we do give animals the benefit of putting them out of their misery, whereas, with humans, it's not always so easy."

"No, it isn't," Bauer agreed. "And you still went into vet school?"

"I loved animals. I wanted to save as many as I could, and yet saving them didn't always necessarily mean keeping them alive. That was something I understood well before I started school, and I think that made it a little easier on me than it was on some of my classmates."

"That isn't an easy thing for anybody," Bauer noted. "And it's not something that you can just turn on and turn off, as something you'll adjust to. So it may have been easier on you, compared to the rest of them, because you were more prepared to look at it a bit differently."

"I think some were already pretty decent with it, but a couple women really struggled with it. They wanted to save everybody, and there is no saving everybody, whether you're working with animals or people," Mags stated. "There comes a point in time when you just can't do anything, and the organic body is done." And, on that very depressing note, she added, with a wry laugh, "It looks like Toby is ready to go back in for the night."

He nodded. "Let's get back to sleep. You've got a long day again tomorrow."

"All my days are long right now," she admitted, with a yawn.

As he stopped to take one last look outside, he froze, seeing something in the distance down below.

"What do you see?" she asked quietly beside him. Her gaze searched the area in the direction he was looking.

"I think I see something, and I need to check it out. Take Toby inside, and lock up tight. Do not come out again, no matter what, and I mean that." With that, he shoved her inside the door, then closed it and waited until he heard the sound of the lock. Then, just like that, he was gone in the darkness.

CHAPTER 6

M AGS WISHED SHE could say that she would watch Bauer, but no windows were on that level that looked out at an angle for her to see where he went. She raced upstairs to a room with a better view, with Toby moving very slowly behind her. Once there, they sat cuddled up together. She wished to God that Bauer hadn't taken off and that it wasn't a last-minute spooky scenario that had sent him running outside. But he had, so now she was stuck with her mind going off in a million directions, wondering where he was and what was happening.

She watched outside the window, wondering if she should have done something more to keep her clinic safe. Her mind had been focused on keeping Toby safe, and that was the right decision. However, now she really didn't want to deal with more damage to the clinic either. As she studied the clinic building, there were no lights or signs of any activity.

She frowned at that, hoping that maybe Bauer had been mistaken. Just then, she thought she heard the door downstairs. Toby growled, and she looked down at him in shock.

"Hey," she whispered, "we have to stay quiet." But that didn't mean Toby was too interested in staying quiet. He stared at the bedroom door, and she nodded. "I know, but, if we leave, we're in trouble," she whispered to him.

Of course Bauer gave her a best-case scenario, but would leaving possibly keep her safer? What if this asshole was out there? When she didn't hear anything else, she wanted to just laugh and relax, until she heard the door rattle again. She texted Bauer. **Sounds like somebody at the door. Is it you?**

He texted back. **No, stay where you are. Stay hidden. I'll be there in a second.**

She hated to even hear that he wasn't right there because *in a second* could mean a whole lot of things, and some weren't good. But she waited, her heart in her throat. She couldn't see the front door, and, of course, that just made it worse. She could only imagine what was going on, and that was ten times more vivid than the probable reality. Still, as she watched Toby, he didn't relax at all. His ears were up, and his lips were curled, showing his teeth.

"Yeah, I hear you," she whispered, "but I really don't want you to get hurt again, buddy." Trouble was, she might not have any choice in the matter this time.

As she watched and waited, she heard a man call out, "Hey, where are you, buddy? It's just me, your friend."

Such an odd tone instilled the guy's words that she stiffened, and Toby started growling again. She tried to shush him, as this man moved through the downstairs of her house.

"Where are you? I checked down at the clinic, but you weren't there, which means you've been cleared to leave. That's perfect, so I came to get you. I heard what happened to you, and I saw that you were carried out of there. That's good. I didn't want you to get hurt. You know that, right?"

She frowned because it sounded like this was a different person entirely from the one who had tried to shoot Toby.

"I'm not sure who saved you," the intruder added. "I was trying. I really was, buddy. You have to know I care."

As the voice moved closer to the stairs, she felt herself backing into the corner by the curtains, her heart in her throat.

"It's okay. It's all right now," he said. "I don't know where you are, but I'll find you. Don't worry."

She heard another sound, then he said, "Shit. Look. I'll be back. Don't worry. I'll be back."

After that, she heard yet another sound and knew he was going out through the glass doors. She wanted to get up and race downstairs, but she also knew that she or Toby might get hurt. Yet this person sounded entirely different from the gunman the other night. Then she heard some caterwauling outside that had her bolting to her feet, with Toby standing at her side. She raced to the window, opened it up, and called out. "He's outside," she screamed. "He's just trying to leave."

Then she heard Bauer's reply. "Nope, he's not going anywhere. I've got him here."

"Can I come down?"

"Sure, you can. I'm calling for backup right now."

And, with that, she raced downstairs to the glass doors, which were already open. Immediately Toby hobbled down and headed outside to the downed man. However, instead of growling, he started to lick the man's face.

"What the hell?" Bauer asked, as he watched Toby. Then the War Dog lay down beside the unconscious man, Toby still looking exhausted, as if he couldn't go any further.

She called Toby back to her. "Obviously Toby knows him," she muttered, her heart in her throat. "I just don't know how or in what way. I don't recognize him at all. And he sure didn't sound like the gunman from the other night either."

"Right, and, until he wakes up, we won't know who he is or how he's involved," Bauer stated. "But that's okay because the cops are on the way, and we've got nothing better to do than sit here and wait for him to wake up again."

She looked over at him. "He didn't sound anything at all like the guy who shot Toby." Then she explained everything that she'd heard him say.

Bauer nodded. "I heard something along that line too, and you're right. It's not the same guy and definitely not the reaction from Toby that we were expecting."

"No," she confirmed. "Obviously Toby knows him. I just don't know how or why."

"No, and that's something else we have to figure out. But that's okay, as we'll just sit here and wait."

Sure enough, the cops arrived within a few minutes, and, once the story was told, an ambulance came because their gunman still hadn't woken up. The cop looked over at Bauer. "What did you hit him with? A steel pipe or something?"

"An intruder came into the house, trying to do God-only-knows what, and you're asking me what I hit him with? I'm not looking for accolades, but I sure don't need to be hassled," Bauer snapped, with a note of disgust. "I don't know who he is, and he's not the same guy as our gunman from the past evening, but our intruder did seem to know Toby. And Toby seems to know the intruder."

The cop frowned. "There's got to be some connection between the dognapping gunman and this guy, so it makes sense that maybe he knew the dog. Maybe he worked with the gunman in the military or something?"

"I don't know about the military connection," Bauer replied, "but I agree with you. There's got to be some connection between this guy and our gunman from the other night."

And, with that, the cop added, "It doesn't matter right now. We've got to get him to the hospital and get his head checked over. He's still unconscious, and it will be easier for everyone if we get him there while he's still alive."

"Maybe so," Bauer conceded, "but I sure hate to have him leave, without getting some answers."

"Well then, maybe you shouldn't have hit him quite so hard," one of the other cops muttered in disgust.

"*Yeah, sure,*" he quipped, turning to face him. "Next time I'll just let him shoot poor Mags here, and then we'll ask her questions when she's dead. How's that?"

The other cop chimed in, "All right, all right, enough already. You're in the clear. We all just want answers."

"Yes, but nobody more than me," Mags announced, stepping forward. "I've been shot at, my clinic broken into. Twice now apparently, and then this guy broke into my house. I don't recognize him at all, not by his voice or by his face, and yet it sounded like he knew exactly where I was, what I was doing, and that Toby was here with me. So, as far as I'm concerned, he's been stalking me too. So I am entitled to some answers, and I want them now."

The cop looked over at her, shrugged, then sighed. "Unless you got a way to wake up this guy, you won't get them right now." And, with that, he gave the okay for the intruder to be loaded up on a gurney and taken into the ambulance.

She turned and looked back at Bauer. "I sure hate to see him leave."

Bauer nodded. "Me too. Once he's at the hospital, we won't get near him anytime soon."

She frowned at Bauer and asked, "So what then? What do we do now?" She hated her sense of helplessness, with things moving well beyond her sense of control.

Bauer stepped closer, pulling her attention away from the ambulance and back to him. "Listen. We'll go back inside, and we'll get some sleep. After that, we'll see. Tomorrow is a whole new day."

MAKING SURE MAGS and Toby had gone back to bed, Bauer checked the house one more time. Something was still not sitting right with him about any of this scenario he'd seen so far. Things just weren't adding up. Then he sent a quick text message to Badger, for him to find when he woke up. After that, Bauer crashed.

He woke up some four hours later, realizing that was all the sleep he would get, but he had functioned on a lot less over the years, so he would do just fine. He heard movement downstairs and noted that Mags was already up and probably preparing to go to work—or potentially worrying about Toby. Bauer hopped up, dressed quickly, and made his way to the kitchen. "There you are. I thought I heard you up and about."

She looked over at him and smiled. "Yeah, once I woke up, it was a hard to keep sleeping, plus Toby here"—she reached down to pet the dog—"was quite restless." Toby's tail thumped in greeting, as he watched Bauer approach.

Bauer bent down and spent a few minutes just petting the dog. "How are you doing, buddy? Not exactly a smooth night, was it?"

"No," she replied, with a sigh. "Pretty upsetting at that."

Bauer nodded. "But we also caught somebody, so it may not be as upsetting as we're thinking."

"Maybe," she murmured. "At the same time we still have a lot of unfinished business here, and we're not out of the woods yet. I mean, I just don't see our intruder being the shooter from the other night."

"No, I don't either. We still have to get to the bottom of this, but at least now maybe we'll have a lead."

She handed him a cup of coffee. "Until then, as far as I'm concerned, this War Dog stays with me, and hopefully the police will have a little more to go on."

"Even if they don't, it will still give Badger and me a whole lot more to go on."

She smiled at that. "I do appreciate that you guys care enough to stick with this."

"We're not done yet. As you mentioned, still an awful lot here is unresolved, and I'm not terribly happy with that." He could see the relief on her face, and he nodded. "I did see the gunman out in the woods, and I'm pretty-darn sure it wasn't our intruder either. His movements were totally different than this guy's. And this guy seemed to be much more happy-go-lucky, from the way he was talking as he looked for the dog."

"I was thinking that too," she said. "When he was inside the house, I mean. And I don't know how he got in the house because all the doors were locked." She looked over at him, her eyebrows raised.

He held up a hand. "I know. Exactly. Plus I locked that door myself. I could see that the lock had been open, and there wasn't any damage."

"Do you think this guy picked the lock?"

Bauer frowned at that. "I can't be sure that he didn't because I don't know what his history is. But there is definitely something off about this whole deal."

"*Off* is right," she declared, with a sigh. "Oh, crap, our visitor told me that he'd checked the clinic. Do you think there is damage?"

"I didn't see any last night. I think what happened is that, while I was checking out the clinic, he was done there and was heading up here. Nothing was broken there this time. I'll be happier when we figure out who he is."

"God, what a nightmare. What do we do now?"

"We'll keep up our guard and keep going as we have been. I'll be at the vet clinic all day today, and I'll probably take Toby out several times, as I check out the perimeter of the clinic, just to make sure that we're not heading into more trouble."

She looked down at the War Dog. "That brings me back to the same question as before. Do you think my staff is in danger?"

"I hope not," he said, "but I can't be sure. And now that the cops have somebody in custody, I'm pretty sure the police will consider this issue mostly dealt with."

She winced at that. "That was my take too," she admitted. "Yet I'm pretty sure, if I had argued with them over closing this case, it wouldn't get me anywhere."

Bauer smiled. "Maybe not, but that doesn't mean we can't continue to figure out what's going on here on our own."

She nodded. "I know, but it just feels … wrong."

"Got it," he agreed cheerfully, as he walked over and refilled his cup of coffee. "I'm glad you got up first. This coffee is great, by the way."

She snorted at that. "It's hard to mess up coffee."

"Oh, I don't know about that. I've seen it done many times."

She chuckled. "You're just trying to make me feel better. Or change the subject."

He grinned. "Is it working?"

"Maybe. Maybe it is." At that, she smiled at him. "We need some breakfast, and then I've got to get down to the office."

He nodded. "Of course you do." When she gave him a questioning look, he shrugged. "I knew you would be going, so that's not a surprise."

"I can't *not* go really, as today is a surgery day. So I'll be very busy. The last thing I need is any interruptions or a gunman around the place," she noted, with a sigh. "I really don't want the cops either, for that matter."

"They could very well come back today," he warned.

"I know. At least the broken window gives me an excuse of what to tell people."

"Good point," he said calmly, as he looked at her. "Are you eating breakfast?"

"I am." She pointed at a bowl of muesli that she was pulling together.

He looked at it, horrified. "Do you mind if I cook something a little more substantial?"

She waved at the kitchen. "Go for it. If you can find it, you're welcome to it."

"Thank you for the hospitality."

She snorted. "Thank you for the guardianship or whatever you want to call it," she added, with another wave of her hand.

"No problem. Besides, we're going on a date one day. Remember?"

"I wondered if you were still thinking along those lines." She gave him a sideways look that he had no trouble interpreting.

"Any reason why I wouldn't be?"

"No. I don't know. I don't really understand men to be honest."

He laughed at that. "We're even. I don't really understand women either."

"Yeah, you do," she argued, with a smile. "I think you have that dialed in more than you're letting on."

"Hell no," he declared a little forcefully. "I just know that I like you."

She snorted. "Is this where I'm supposed to say, *I like you too?*"

His grin flashed at her. "Maybe, I mean, only if you really mean it."

"*Humph.* I'll have to give it some thought. Anyway, let's just keep moving forward and keep our eyes focused on this guy today." She smiled, her hand reaching down to Toby, who stood next to her, his tail once again wagging. "I'll start with checking his wounds and changing the bandage when I get to the clinic." She frowned, looking at it now. "It's bled a bit overnight."

Still smiling from their thinly veiled flirting, Bauer said, "Of course it's been bleeding. He's not supposed to be moving around, is he?"

"It would be better if we'd kept him crated, so he would rest more, but I know he hates it. I'm trying to keep him alive, and the thought of him being cornered in a crate, with somebody trying to shoot him, makes me sick. I just can't do it," she explained. "And believe me. I already feel guilty enough."

"You don't need to feel guilty at all," he reiterated. "You're doing what you can, and honestly, given the circumstances, that's a lot. Actually last night, when all that was happening, I was really glad Toby wasn't crated, so he could protect you, if it came down to it."

"I thought that too. God, what a mess. Toby should be safe at work during the day though, right?" She looked over at Bauer, and he realized just how insecure she was feeling about it all.

"Yes, and I'll be there all day today," he stated. "And, since you'll be in surgery, I'll take care of Toby, so you don't have to worry about him."

"I get that's supposed to make me feel better, but I would feel far better if you had something to say about the gunman not being there to make trouble today."

"I don't know that to be true, and I won't lie to you."

She winced. "Right. Of course you won't. But can I say that I wouldn't mind if you did, just to give me the tiniest bit of reassurance?"

"Sorry, but, in a case like this, I think we're all better off if we stay alert."

And, with that, she sat back down and finished eating her breakfast.

Checking out the fridge, he pulled out bacon and eggs and started cooking.

A few minutes later she murmured, "I'm amazed at how comfortable you are in the kitchen."

"Lots of years of living alone," he replied.

"I get that, but I'm in the same boat and not nearly as fast or as proficient as you are."

"I didn't spend so many years going to school and then building a business either," he added, with a smirk. "You know we can't do it all, so, when we focus on one thing, we give up a little bit of something else in order to make it happen."

"I don't even want to think about having given up anything, but you're right. I gave up a lot really. I haven't regretted it, but that choice certainly has impacted other things in my life."

"Like relationships?" he asked.

"Sure, relationships are part of it, no doubt."

He poured himself a third cup of coffee, when he sat down with his breakfast. "Thank you for not getting up and taking off to work."

"I figured you wouldn't let me walk there alone with Toby. Plus you went to all that trouble with your breakfast."

He laughed. "That was very considerate, thank you. That's a good sign."

"Maybe," she conceded, "but that doesn't mean we should be dating."

He looked at her over his cup of coffee. "Nervous much?"

She shrugged.

"It comes down to trust, you know?" he stated.

"Yeah, and I haven't been very good at that. Not since ..." Then she let her voice trail off.

"Me too," he agreed. "I figured that maybe we could take that journey together."

"What makes you think I'm interested?" His gaze twinkled, as he watched the color move up her cheeks. "Fine, forget it. I just—"

"I know. And I would never want you to feel pressured,

but I don't think either one of us is doing all that great on our own."

She stared at him in shock. "What do you mean? I'm doing just fine."

He nodded. "At least as far as your professional life goes, sure. Me too. But honestly do you want to be alone for the rest of your life?"

After a few moments of silently staring at him, she admitted, "No. ... I just hadn't really expected to be heading down this pathway right now."

"I don't think it ever comes to us when we're ready. I'm just asking you to be open enough to see if something's here that we both want." He could see that she wanted to say something more, but eventually she just closed her mouth. Somehow he felt like it was a missed opportunity. "The one thing you can always do, no matter how this goes, is talk to me."

She nodded slowly. "Maybe at the end of the day, I'll feel a little bit more like I can talk to you. At the moment I just feel mentally, physically, and emotionally exhausted, and I don't really trust myself."

"I get that," he said, with a wry smile. "We're both a little overwhelmed at the moment."

"I can't envision you ever overwhelmed. You appear to have picked up and handled all this with a serious assurance that I can only admire."

He chuckled. "Experience does count sometimes."

"Maybe," she conceded, "and maybe that's where the nerves are from—on the whole dating thing."

He studied her, remaining silent, letting her share.

"Outside of the one partner, I don't have a whole lot of experience with all this emotional stuff," she shared. "I used to always just hide away, rather than deal with it. I figured that that was the reason he chose someone else."

"And do you really think it was, or do you think it was more about your work?"

"I don't know." She frowned. "He knew I was a workaholic. I guess I expected him to understand. But I guess he thought that, when we got married, I would ease back and would spend a lot more time with him. In the end, he felt the need to sabotage our relationship by sleeping with my best friend and getting caught, just before the wedding. I should have seen that coming and maybe done something different."

"What? So somehow you think you're solely responsible?"

She slowly lowered her coffee cup, then looked at him. "What if I am? I could totally mess it up again."

He shook his head. "Hey, remember that part about no pressure? Let's just have dinner."

"Technically we've already had a steak dinner," she noted, pointing around her kitchen.

He grinned. "And we both survived. Imagine that." She flushed. "I'm not mocking you," he added. "I just think it's important, if this is something you want to check out a little further, that we invest the time and energy to see if anything is there between us."

"Yet, as you mentioned"—her tone wry—"obviously something is between us already. The question is whether or not we're both open to making some kind of commitment."

"I am," he stated.

She sighed and shook her head. "Are you sure you want to do this right now?"

He nodded. "You know, if Badger had told me that this

was waiting for me on this assignment, I would have run in the opposite direction. I might have even said something along those lines to him," Bauer admitted. "I get that we don't have anything waiting for us right now," he admitted, with a smile, "because, in your mind, we still aren't there."

She nodded. "And it doesn't feel that we're getting anywhere. And that's because we're so focused on Toby here, and all that's going on around us, which is good. That's where our focus needs to be. At least for now."

"I don't disagree with that at all," Bauer added, "but also other things are going on between us—for me anyway, maybe not for you. There can be a risk and potentially a hard pill to swallow, but I really want to check this out. But if you don't, … and again, no pressure, if you don't, and if you know that, then maybe it would be best if you just said so now," he suggested, staring at her over his coffee cup.

"Would you believe me?" she asked, with a wry look.

He laughed out loud. "As it turns out, I'm very good at reading body language, so the answer to that question would be no," he declared. "In that case, I would have to take no to really mean that you're just not ready to handle a relationship."

"And yet?" She stared at him. "You're right. We're both hiding. So, what in the hell made you decide to come out of hiding at this particular time?" she asked, with a good note of humor in her voice.

"Because it's making me deal with things I wasn't really thinking I could deal with. And again we don't really get a choice sometimes," he noted, his own smile bright. "I guess that it's seeing you here, with Toby, seeing a woman, someone I respect and really want to spend more time with." he explained. "I really didn't expect something like this to just happen out of the blue, but here it is. So I'm stepping out of my bubble to see if it's something of interest for you as well."

"Which, as you already know, it is." But she gave him a good frown, as if upset that he had pushed the issue.

He just frowned right back. She burst out laughing, and he nodded. "See? We understand each other quite well."

"Maybe, but opening those floodgates ..."

"But how much of the time are those floodgates only closed because it's a habit? Because it's comfortable? Because it's something we allowed at the time? Because it was too painful to deal with whatever shit we were going through? But we just continue to keep that door closed, don't we?"

"Some people go out and jump right back on the horse," she admitted, "but apparently we didn't."

"No, we didn't, and I think that's because, when we care, we care deeply, and, when we got hurt, we got hurt deeply."

She slowly nodded. "I can't argue that because it's true, and it definitely wouldn't have been easy getting back on the horse in the way people normally do. So, I just buried myself in work instead. And apparently you did too."

He smiled. "More or less, then my accident happened not all that long afterward, and that set me back quite a bit more."

"I don't have that as an excuse," she noted, staring at him. "I just basically decided that I wouldn't even bother anymore."

"Because it was easier. It's easier to just ignore it all, but it doesn't necessarily help us down the road. If that single life isn't what we want for ourselves down the road, then we must take a chance."

"I wonder if it's that easy," she murmured, staring at him.

"Why don't we take that step and find out?"

She laughed. "Pretty sure I already said yes."

"Pretty sure I'm still looking for a little more enthusiasm." But the look that he caught was the one that made the most sense. She was so confident, so secure in so many areas of her world and in her life and so ready to jump up for the animals, but, when it came to relationships, she'd fallen hard and had taken the hurt deep. That he could understand. "Mags, I promise that hurting you is not on the books."

"But if I do decide that I like you," she began, flashing a wicked grin his way, "and it doesn't work out, I'll still get hurt, even if you don't mean to."

"Are you going to hide for your whole life because of that?"

"It's been working so far," she declared, as she got up. Then she walked over and washed her coffee cup and put it on the side of the counter. She looked back at him, and he could see the guardedness still in her gaze. "But you're right. Definitely something is between us. So I'm willing to give it a chance and see where it goes."

"And can you withhold judgment if it doesn't go perfectly?" he asked her.

She stared at him, as she considered his question. "I guess that's kind of the next thing, isn't it?"

He nodded. "I don't really want to be judged against whatever milestone this other guy left you with."

She frowned at that thought. "I hadn't considered that," she noted, going silent for a bit. Then with a nod, she added, "You're right. That's not fair for either of us. I don't want to be judged based on the woman you had in your life either."

"Good," he said, with a bright smile. "In that case, we'll both start fresh and do our best to keep it that way, right?"

"*Sure*," she quipped, with an eyeroll. "You make it sound so easy."

"You know what? I have an idea that, for the two of us, it could be really easy." Heading to the sink, he washed his plate, then added, "Come on. Let's get back to work."

At that, she laughed. "Wow, you'll be as much of a workaholic as I am."

"Too late," he pointed out. "That's partly why I understand what makes you tick."

"I'm glad somebody does."

"Oh, you understand perfectly well. You feel alive when you're with the animals," he noted. "And, so far, you might not have met anybody else who shared the same depths of caring for these animals—or for you, in fact. I get it. Believe me. There's nothing quite like being with somebody who doesn't care as much as you do, to make you feel like you're unlovable and not worthy."

"God, all that stuff was just so hard," she murmured, staring at him. "To even think about going back down that pathway is terrifying."

"I know," he agreed. "I was there too. Remember?"

She nodded, then looked down at Toby. With a big grin for him, she said, "Come on, Toby. Apparently it's time to get to work, so we'll walk down there together." Then looking to Bauer, she asked, "When do you want to do dinner?"

"You mean, besides tonight?"

She nodded. "I presume we're not talking anytime soon and will wait until this mess is over."

"Either way, I'll be right here beside you the whole time

until it is. So how about this weekend?"

She stared at him. "Do you really think we'll have answers that soon?"

Such hope filled her voice that he had to laugh. "I figured if I don't give you a deadline and an actual date on the calendar, you might back out on me. Thus this is my attempt at locking you in." She frowned at him, and he nodded, understanding her reluctance. "And I said, *No pressure*, didn't I?"

"Yeah, but that didn't last long," she muttered, but no rancor was in her tone.

He smiled. "I'm cooking dinner tonight, so for now how about the weekend for our dinner date?"

"Maybe the weekend," she conceded, with a short nod. "We'll see where we are—at that point." And, with that, they headed toward the clinic.

CHAPTER 7

M AGS FELT A weird sensation all day, always expecting
to see or to hear something wrong throughout the
day. But when nothing happened, she was relieved, yet
almost disappointed. There was a kind of flatness to the day,
a sense of letdown. She wanted answers, and she wanted
them badly, but apparently nobody was inclined to give
them to her. She had asked Bauer during the day if he'd
heard anything from the cops, but he just shook his head.
She looked at him for more, but people were waiting for her,
so she asked in mild desperation, "Can you find out?"

With that, he nodded, then headed out to the backyard.

He'd stayed close all day, and she appreciated that. He'd
even come in with coffee once or twice and had insisted that
she stop and take a quick break and eat something. She'd
grumbled at him the whole time, but he stood there, stoic,
ignoring her arguments.

Yet she had quickly plowed through the food and realized that she was much better for it. When she had gotten up
and tossed away the garbage, she looked over at him. "How
did you know?"

"You were starting to get a little snappy," he replied.

She gave him an eyeroll. "I doubt anybody else would
use that term."

"No, I think *pissed off and angry* is what I heard bantered around," he stated, with a bright smile.

"You're kidding."

"Not kidding, sorry."

She sighed. "It's this waiting. I mean, I get that it's supposed to be overwhelming, and now that someone was caught, everybody is expecting me to be happy and settled, so who cares about answers," she explained, "but it doesn't feel right."

"Oh, I agree with you there," he confirmed. "Badger and I are doing what we can, and I've got phone calls into the cops as well. Plus Badger is trying to get a history on our intruder from last night, and we're looking for some background on all of it. However, so far, I don't have anybody getting back to me, which typically means they don't have squat."

Her shoulders slumped. "I guess that's fair enough."

"You keep focused on your day. I'll stay focused on Toby and on getting answers," he reminded her. "Rest assured, the cops haven't forgotten about us, and somebody will get back to us, as soon as they have something."

"Do you think so?" she asked, looking at him strangely. "I figured maybe they're hoping if they ignore us long enough, we'll just go away."

"That's not happening," Bauer declared. "So just hold down the fort and stay strong. Hopefully we'll get some answers by the end of the day."

With that, she pretended to be happy with it. He was right. Until somebody got back to them, there wasn't much they could do but stay the course. Nearing the end of the day she walked past the reception room and noted it was empty. She turned to look at her receptionist and saw Sarah already packing up. "Are we done?" Mags asked hopefully.

"Absolutely. You were caught up in surgery for so much of it that I don't even think you saw half of the people who came through here."

"The surgeries were relatively light," Mags shared. "A few stitches here and there, a couple cysts, a biopsy, an ear hematoma repair. Thankfully nothing major."

"I'm glad to hear that," Sarah said. "You were definitely not yourself." Mags frowned at her friend and assistant, and Sarah nodded. "You know it yourself."

"I do know it," she admitted. "Plus Bauer even mentioned I was *snappy*."

"You haven't exactly been getting a whole lot of sleep."

"Exactly."

"But tomorrow is a new day, and hopefully, with some sleep tonight, you'll be back to normal."

"That's the plan," Mags agreed, with a smile. She walked behind Sarah as she left, locked up the front door behind her, then set the alarm for the front and headed into the back. She had Toby and one other patient, who'd been in for a fairly minor surgery. However, the owners had an emergency and couldn't pick her up at the end of the day, sending word that they would come in the morning to get Millie.

So, it was a simple case of just needing a safe place to stay. The War Dog was awake and happy and now would be content to just curl up in the corner of the house with Mags. Since Toby was coming home with her, so would Millie. Before she set the alarm for the back area, she turned to see Bauer standing there.

He waved around the clinic. "I guess it doesn't make much difference if you stay here or not."

"I normally stay if I'm worried about a surgical patient,"

she replied, looking at him crossly. "In this case I'm not concerned at all. It was a routine procedure, and Millie is ready to go home. However, her owners couldn't come and collect her tonight. But I'm uncomfortable with leaving her here, under the circumstances. Otherwise I would come down in a couple hours to check on her and again in the wee hours of the morning."

"Do you sleep better at home than here?" Bauer asked.

"I do. Much better. Yet, if I thought anything was to worry about with Millie, believe me. I would be staying here."

"*You* wouldn't," he argued. "*I* would." She glared at him, and he just shrugged. "Some things have to be done the way they have to be done."

She muttered, "I'm sure that means something to you, but it sure doesn't to me."

He laughed at her, not even trying to explain it. "Are you ready to go home?"

She nodded. "I'm hungry again," she announced.

"That's good because I'm cooking dinner again."

"Right," she noted. "That's a good thing. Otherwise I'd be ordering something in right now, so I could take it home from here." When he frowned at that detail, she explained, "Deliveries often get confused between the clinic and my house. Sometimes the delivery people just take the easy out and the shortest route and deliver it here. So it's just way easier to wait here for it to come. However, if that were the case tonight, I should have ordered it a while ago. If I was alone, I would have just stayed and worked in the office."

"But you're not doing that tonight," Bauer stated, his tone inflexible. She glared at him once more, and he smiled right back. "Come on. Let's collect the two dogs and go up to the house."

She nodded and walked outside and headed back up to the house, with Toby moving slowly at her side. Millie was on a leash held by Bauer. She was happy to be out of her cage too. As Mags walked beside Toby, checking his gait, she had to acknowledge that he was finally doing somewhat better. "He's doing pretty decent," she murmured to Bauer. "I spent an hour going over his bandages and checking on his lab tests, and I think he's holding up okay."

"He looks to be just fine," Bauer noted. "I'm really surprised he's moving as well as he is."

"I think that's sheer stubbornness on his part," she suggested. "I've done amputations where they weren't this mobile, not like Toby is. In his case, I don't know whether it's because of what he already went through or what. I don't know, but he's been pretty quick to get up on his feet and go."

Bauer nodded. "I imagine not all animals are the same, just like people aren't the same."

"That's true," she agreed, "and we do try to keep an eye on everyone, but Toby's exceptional, and he consistently surprises me."

"I like hearing that he's doing better than you expect."

"Maybe, but it still worries me that he's overdoing it though."

"He's only been on his feet a little while when we had him outside to go to the bathroom a couple times today," Bauer argued. "I don't think that's been too much for him."

"No, you're right," she conceded. "I just don't want him to have a setback."

"I'm with you on that, so we'll just do the best we can. If he needs to go back in a crate, he will. He won't like it much, but I can see that it might make you feel better."

"How sad is that," she muttered. "I would worry more if I saw any fresh bleeding. Actually he's using the other legs, and all the bleeding has stopped. The stump is showing decent healing. It's the drainage I was worried about, but I cleaned all that out, and it's looking pretty good."

Bauer nodded. "As somebody who went through an amputation myself, I understand the process. I understand how quickly we can heal, and I also understand how easy it is to do too much and to slow down that healing."

She didn't know what to say about any of that. He rarely mentioned anything about his accident or his injuries. "Are you missing much?" she asked cautiously.

"Initially half a foot," he shared, "and, damn, if that didn't make me feel like it's only half an injury. However, the infection wouldn't heal, so they ended up taking off more of the leg, not quite to the knee."

That raised her eyebrow. "The trouble is, even missing half a foot essentially means learning to walk all over again," she added, looking at Toby, as if trying to process it in her own head. "It's amazing just how much we need that pad, the sole, the whole front section of the foot for balance. The toes, for grip, gait, … just to walk properly. Of course, from your perspective, even now with more of the leg gone, you probably still think that it's a minor injury in comparison to your war buddies and that you should have been through rehab faster."

"Exactly," he replied, with a laugh. "However, there for a while, the docs were talking about taking off more of my leg if they couldn't get the infection to go away. Thankfully I got lucky, and that worked out. Also, because of the work I used to do, I have this tough guy image to maintain, and it just didn't sit right that something like missing a foot should hold me back so much."

"And, in another instance, maybe it wouldn't have. It also depends on what other injuries you were dealing with at the same time that may have influenced the overall amount of downtime."

"Quite a few. I had a ruptured spleen, a punctured lung, a broken femur rebuilt with rods, a couple broken ribs, half a rib missing, plus my hand—lost part of it too. Thankfully it's not my dominant hand. Still Kat thinks I would like to have a prosthetic, and she's working on that." She stopped in her tracks and stared at him. He gave her a quirky smile. "As I mentioned, a few other injuries."

"Jeez," she muttered, under her breath. "You're lucky to be alive."

"I am, and, as you pointed out, that may be one of the reasons I decided to venture down this whole relationship path again—although I was in hard denial, until Toby went missing, and I saw you again."

At that, she glared at him.

"What? Did you think I would forget about our upcoming dinner date?" he teased, laughing at her.

"I was hoping you wouldn't push quite so much."

"Not pushing, just saying it out loud and trying to get you a little more comfortable with the whole concept. Trying to make the unfamiliar more familiar."

"It's not working," she stated gruffly.

"Yeah, but I think, for you, a lot of it is just habit."

"What? This is a habit? Other than you, I don't have men asking me out. So how the hell do you figure that?"

"Because, outside of the insecurity and the sense of distrust that somebody might hurt you again, I'm not sure how much of what you're feeling is because you've locked down the initial pain and eventually just kept it down, out of sight. So much so that, when I brought it up, you didn't even know how to respond."

"Of course I didn't know how to respond," she snapped, as they made the last little way up to her house. "How can I respond when I wasn't expecting it? I've never been very good at hiding my feelings."

"Good," he replied, "because I'm not either."

She frowned at him. "I would have said that you have a hell of a poker face. I can't read it at all."

"Never." He shook his head. "No, I fail at poker, and everybody seems to read my face just fine. In your case, I think you're trying *not* to read it."

That stopped her in her tracks. "That sounds an awful lot like you expect me to respond in some way that I don't even know how to respond. And makes me feel like I'm in the wrong, and I hate that."

He shook his head. "I'm not expecting you to respond in any particular way," he replied gently. "I'm just looking for honesty between us."

"Fine," she said, raising both hands in surrender. "*Honestly* this conversation is making me uncomfortable."

"Okay, so we'll change it," he replied immediately. Then, sure enough, he did. "Did you sense or feel anything going on around you today at the clinic?"

She unlocked her front door, then stepped inside, letting Toby step in just ahead of her. As she went to take another step, Bauer slammed an arm straight across her chest and quietly said, "Wait!"

BAUER WATCHED TOBY, as his ears went back and his lip curled. "Stay here," he whispered to Mags. Bauer reached down and unhooked the leash on Toby, and, with a finger to his lips, he stepped forward, sliding along the wall, until he could get close enough to see around the corner.

And saw ... nothing. The house was in shadows, so it was just dark enough to impede his vision. He waited until his eyes adjusted, and, as he stepped forward, he heard Toby at his side, moving stealthily. He reached his fingers down, but it was too late, as a man spoke.

"There you are, you little bastard."

Bauer pulled Toby back, just as a shot rang out from the far end of the house and hit the corner of the nearby wall. He heard the startled shriek from Mags behind him, as he pushed Toby back to her, handed her Millie's leash, and told her to get down to the clinic.

Clipping the leash back on Toby, she whispered, "I'm not leaving you."

"Yes, you are," he argued quietly. "I'll try and draw him out, but, if he thinks he's pinned, he'll just shoot his way out. Go down and call the cops."

"I can do that from outside." He gave her a hard look, as she raised her hands and stepped back outside again.

Bauer returned his attention to the silence in the living room. "The dog is not here."

"It was," snapped the other man. "The damn thing needs shooting."

"Why is that? What did he ever do to you?"

"Bit me," he snapped. "Dogs like that, they're dangerous as hell. You can't let a dog like that live. He's a menace."

"He's just a dog. One you probably kicked and pro-voked into biting you. Still, I don't know why you've gone to such lengths to try and kill him."

"I won't explain it to you," he spat, "but I can tell you one thing. If he gets in my way again, I'll make sure it's not just the dog that gets a bullet."

"Wow, threats now. That's great. You're already breaking into her house, and here you are making threats on top of it. Isn't it enough that we already have one guy in custody?"

"Yeah, well, I'll be fixing that too," he declared, with a sneer. Then he let out a barrage of firepower that kept chipping off the corner of the wall. Behind the rapid-fire cover, Bauer thought he heard odd sounds, and swore, thinking the guy had bolted outside, but which way would he go?

He can't go to the clinic. Bauer had just sent Mags down there with the two dogs, and that wasn't cool. Bauer had to make a calculated decision. Rather than heading anywhere, he raced out around the front of the house and checked to see where the gunman was, but he saw nobody headed to the clinic. With that in mind, Bauer bolted around the back of the house, which led to the more forested areas, basically a half-wild section where the gunman would have lots of cover. Bauer couldn't see him, but he heard someone thundering through the brush.

Bauer raced after him, needing to get a visual or at least some detail to help ID this guy, but, so far, Bauer was too far behind because he'd been more worried about this gunman going after Mags and the War Dog at the clinic. Cursing his inability to run fast in the darkness through the trees, he picked up as much speed as he could. He tried his best, forcing his body to pump out as much power as possible. Just as he came around a bend, the gunman threw himself into an old pickup truck and ripped off down the road.

Bauer couldn't get a license plate, but he got the color and model of the truck. He quickly phoned Badger. "A gunman broke into her house and has just left here. He's driving an old gray Toyota pickup, coming down off the back road and turning onto the main road. He was too far away for me to get a license plate."

Badger muttered, "I'm on it."

With that, Bauer disconnected and retraced his steps, moving at a somewhat slower pace, but still at a pretty good clip, in case that damn vehicle headed to the clinic. Bauer kept it in sight, but thankfully it headed off on the main road and disappeared.

As soon as he reached the clinic, the door opened ahead of him, and Mags bolted out, throwing her arms around him. "Who the hell was that?" she cried out.

"That was somebody in your house, waiting for the War Dog to come back," Bauer murmured, holding her close. He pulled her tighter against him and whispered to her, trying to calm her nerves. "It's okay. You're fine."

She reared back and glared at him. "I'm fine, but you could have been shot."

He stared at her and realized that she had been worried about him, not just about herself or Toby. He grinned at her, a slow blooming smile that was both cheeky and absolutely delighted. "*Ha*. You were worried about me. Go ahead. Admit it."

"Of course I was worried about you," she snapped at him. Finally, not being able to calm her nerves, she raised both hands in the air, palms up. "Although *why*, I don't know, since you keep throwing yourself into these scenarios."

"*Sure*," he admitted, with a smug tone. "Got to keep my

girlfriend safe." And, with that, he looped an arm around her shoulders and pulled her back toward the clinic and the dogs.

But she stopped, midstep. "*Girlfriend?*" She added an ominous tone to that word.

He chuckled. "Yep, surely that's obvious by now." At that, he looked around. "Do you want to go back up to the house or stay down here?"

"Home. Plus I need to see if he did any damage. … And you still haven't explained the *girlfriend* remark."

"No explanation needed," he said, as he beamed at her. "You're doing really well on this new pathway of ours."

"I'm not doing well at all. Sounds to me like you're pushing. *Again.*"

"Nope, not at all," he disagreed. "Absolutely *not* pushing."

"But you are." She glared at him in protest.

"I mean, so what if I called you my girlfriend? How is that pushing? Surely it's not more than you can handle."

"No, it's not. I mean, I'm still struggling, but you apparently are jumping into this with both feet." She just turned and stared at him.

He reached out and clicked her jaw shut and smiled. "The dogs, remember?"

She glared at him, then headed back to the cages.

He watched while she checked over Millie, who was more than anxious to be petted. She looked down at her and shook her head. "I don't feel that good about leaving Millie here alone but not sure the house is any better after the gunman …"

"Let's just take them both back up to the house then."

With the dogs on leashes, she asked, "Are we even allowed to go in?"

"We are, but we will have company soon. The cops are on the way."

Her shoulders sagged. "So, another evening where I not only don't get dinner on time but we'll have to deal with them."

"Sorry." By the time they got up to the house, he heard the sirens in the distance.

She sighed. "We could have had dinner first. They didn't seem in any hurry when I called."

"Badger probably leaned on them."

"*Great*, so he already knows too. Why don't you just post it in the dailies?"

"Hey, I would if I thought it would do any good. You shouldn't be upset because people will know eventually anyway."

"I'm trying to run a business. It's hardly a vote of confidence when gunmen are around every corner. It's been what, the third time in the last week? I've lost count."

"We're doing everything we can to get this back on track."

"I know. It's just frustrating."

He led the way back up to the house. When Mags stood inside and saw all the damage—the drywall, bits of paint and wall debris all over her floor—she stopped and stared. "Now you'll tell me that I can't even clean this up, won't you?"

"Not until the cops see it first," he noted. "This is probably enough damage to warrant an insurance claim too, so you might want to refrain from doing much."

"I don't know. If I don't have to file a claim, I would prefer not to. I don't like dealing with them either. The deductibles are often so high that it's not even worth it."

"Still you might want to take some photos before the cops arrive and shoo us away. I'll take a good look in a few minutes. We'll have to deal with the cops first anyway." He could see how little she wanted to deal with anything, but it wasn't something she could avoid at this point. Back in the kitchen, he quickly put on coffee for everybody. By the time she brought the cops through, and they had taken a look at the damage, Bauer noted two of them, one on the phone and the other one looking over at him.

"I see we have a problem," the cop stated.

"What problem is that?"

"You didn't catch the one guy who we could have gotten answers from."

"No, I didn't." There was nothing to like about the cop's tone or words. "You still have another one in custody though, don't you?"

"He's in hospital right now," he replied, "still with a head injury."

"But he's conscious?"

"He's conscious, but he's got a concussion, so they're erring on the side of caution, keeping him in for a bit."

"And what? He doesn't have anything to say?"

The cop hesitated. "He appears to be under the care of a psychiatrist, but the patient's not considered dangerous in any way."

At that, Bauer nodded. "That kind of makes sense. He was concerned about the dog. Looking back at it, I don't think he was intent on coming after us," Bauer admitted. "Now this gunman today, that was a completely different story. He was shooting at whatever he could hit, but basically he hated the dog."

Mags stepped into the kitchen right then, and Bauer

wished he'd kept his voice down.

"Seriously? That War Dog has done nothing to anyone," Mags proclaimed.

"I'm not even sure that this was necessarily the dog he was trying to shoot," the cop added.

Bauer shook his. "The shooter was so angry tonight that the War Dog was *definitely* the target, but he was for shooting *any* animal. Possibly us too."

Mags stared at him, her eyes widening. "What? What? You mean somebody is just associating *all* dogs with this one and thinks *all* should be taken out? And we're associated with it too?"

"Something like that. He told me that Toby bit him."

"And yet I don't know when," she said defensively. "It would have been before he came to me, like two weeks ago— unless he was the one who broke in and dognapped him— because Toby hasn't been close enough to anybody else to bite them. Well, other than you, Bauer, as you carried Toby back to the clinic, after after he was shot out in the woods."

"Exactly," Bauer agreed, and he turned to the cop. "I need to finish my research on the guy in the hospital, so we can find this buddy of his. They have to be connected."

The cop didn't like anything about it. "Look. I would suggest that you just stay out of it. Let us handle this. I don't know what you did in the military, and I get that you think you have a personal stake in this, but you guys really need to butt out. And we'll tell Badger the same thing."

"You go ahead and do that, but I disagree. You have made zero progress, and I am not sure you even took the dognapping seriously at all. I don't want that War Dog or the vet shot."

At that, Mags walked closer to Bauer.

"Meaning, what?" the cop asked.

Bauer tucked her up closer to him. "At this point in time, I'm more concerned with catching the gunman who broke in and shot up the house today."

"So am I," the cop replied. "Obviously it's a different kettle of fish than the one who's in the hospital. The question is, are these men related? I've seen both of them, and they don't look similar."

"That doesn't mean that they don't have different fathers or mothers or maybe were adopted even," Bauer suggested, turning to look at her. "I just find it difficult to believe that two separate cases against this same War Dog aren't related somehow." He looked over at the cop to see him nodding.

"Agreed."

Bauer looked back at her and said, "Maybe we should go *out* for dinner tonight."

She shook her head. "I'm not leaving the dogs."

Bauer looked down at Toby and Millie and nodded. "Okay. Maybe we'll order in then."

She laughed, looking at him incredulously. "I'm not sure how you can even think about eating right now, but that sounds like what my plan was originally."

Bauer looked over at the cop. "Presumably you need access to all this?"

He nodded. "Yeah, we have a team coming in. They'll check for fingerprints and grab any bullets and casings they can find, plus look for footprints and anything else we see around here."

Bauer nodded.

"It would be better if you left," the cop noted, looking over at Mags.

"That's not happening," Bauer replied. "You shouldn't

need the kitchen, so I can always whip up a meal, and we can eat it upstairs on the deck." Mags turned to him, and he saw the gratitude in her gaze. "That's what we'll do. Why don't you take the dogs on up, Mags, and I'll bring up the food in a little while."

"I can help with dinner," she offered.

"Don't worry about it. I got dinner. You wanted to shower after all the surgeries today, so why don't you just go up and chill."

She laughed. "You make a great housemate."

"Yep, I do. Now go."

She rolled her eyes, then looked at the cop and asked, "You don't need me, right?"

"I'll need you to sign a statement, but we can do that up on the deck right now, if you want."

"Sure, let's go get that done," she agreed, and she led the way upstairs.

At that, Bauer checked out the other cop, who had stepped into the kitchen doorway. Bauer shifted his hands to his hips at the expression on the cop's face. "What the hell aren't you guys telling me?"

"It doesn't look like the lock on the door was picked."

"What?"

"The guy used a key to get in."

CHAPTER 8

BY THE TIME dinner was done, Mags felt some of the adrenaline and the shock fading away. "I'm so tired now," she murmured, struggling to hold back her yawn. "And look. The cops still haven't left."

"No, they haven't, and they'll probably be a little while yet, but I can't imagine it will be that much longer," he noted. "Do you want to go to bed?"

She shook her head. "I won't sleep while they're in the house."

"Maybe not, but I'll be staying up anyway, and it doesn't make sense that you should too."

"Why?" she asked. He hesitated, while she glared at him. "Don't even think about hiding something from me."

"Okay, but you'll just have to deal with the problem though."

"What problem is that?"

"The gunman didn't break into the house. The cops suspect he had a key. Or you left it unlocked."

She sat back and stared at him. "How the hell would he have a key to my house?"

"It's possible that he got a hold of your keys and had one made. It's also possible he picked it. Who knows? There's all kinds of ways to get in, clearly not necessarily lawful ways of course."

Her breath rushed out. as she assimilated this news. "That really sucks. I was just starting to think that maybe this would be over soon. Now you had to throw that one at me."

"I'm sorry. I wasn't in a big hurry to tell you that. At least, if he had busted into the house, we would know he got in by force. Obviously that's not an ideal scenario either, but it's better than thinking that he had a key. So, I'll be staying up tonight, and I've already got an emergency call in to get a locksmith out here. Depending on when he calls me back, we'll know if he can come tonight or not."

"*Right*," she muttered, her breath slowly returning to normal. "I can't imagine how he got a copy of my key though."

"Did you lose your purse recently or anything like that?"

She frowned. "I don't remember losing my bag at all. I have misplaced it a time or two," she admitted. "Like today, but, with all we have going on, I thought nothing of it. Besides, Sarah and I found it again."

"Where was it?"

"Near the reception desk but back a ways on the floor."

Bauer nodded. "So does Sarah ever step away from the reception area?"

Mags grimaced. "We are shorthanded. And, yes, she goes to get coffee or to make a bathroom run or to get a file off my desk to help with a caller or even to get paper for the fax machine or whatever. It happens. Plus today was surgery day, so I was tied to the back area. Sarah was keeping track of the front area. We were both doing the best we could in our solo duties."

"So, it's plausible that, if the shooter was in there be-cause of a pet or a fake question or whatever, he somehow distracted Sarah or just waited for her to leave her post. When he saw the purse, he must have checked it for keys and made an impression. If he had the clay on him, he would not even need to leave with them, could put the purse right back. Even without the clay, he could just scan the key image. Takes seconds. Put the purse right back where he found it. Or nearby at least. No one would be the wiser. Then he could have a duplicate made to match his impression or the scan."

"Plausible, yes, but that shows some preplanning. Why would he do that?"

"I don't know, but, depending on his background records, it could be that he just wasn't capable of *not* taking advantage of an opportunity like that," Bauer suggested. "Yet we don't know that either."

"Jeez. I'll have to ask Sarah about that."

"So, think back. Did you have any kind of problem with a client a few months ago, give or take?" She stared at him and shook her head slowly, then her head suddenly stopped.

He nodded. "Now we're getting somewhere."

"Oh my God," she gasped. "It wouldn't be him, would it?"

"You tell me. You've seen and heard some people, and so far, you didn't think any of them were the same guy you had here a few days ago."

"No," she said, frowning, "at least I don't think so, but honestly some of this is becoming a bit of a blur."

"So, the trouble a few months ago. What happened?"

"His dog died. It had been shot, and he brought it in, saying it had bit him. The way I remember his story, the dog was aggressive, so he kept it in. But somehow it had gotten into the neighbors' yard, and the neighbors had shot it, apparently afraid for their life. He brought the dog in, but I couldn't save it," she said, her hands out, palms up. "It was already too badly hurt, with all kinds of injuries. One bullet had damaged the lungs, and one eye was in ruins. But the owner, he got quite angry at me."

"What are the chances that he shot the dog himself?"

"But then why bring him into me?" She frowned. "Although I'm not sure it was the dog's owner who brought it in."

At that, Bauer nodded. "Bingo."

She looked at him in shock. "There's no *bingo* to this at all," she snapped. "I don't get it."

"Yeah, probably not that guy from two months ago. No, but here, we have two friends, brothers, family, or something. The one kills, then the other one brings them in to save them, and you've got the same scenario again. One's trying to save the dog you've got, while the other one's trying to kill it. We just have to find out who the hell they are."

NOT UNTIL THE next morning did Bauer finally get some information in. With the name of the guy still in the hospital, Bauer finally had a way of begin to put names to the actors he had encountered so far. This guy in the hospital, Ken, had no siblings, no family, not as far as anybody could see. Badger was working on it, trying to get as much information as they could find. Meanwhile, Bauer had contacted the cops and had told them about his theory, but the cop had been pretty clear about Bauer staying out of it.

No way. Bauer knew this gunman would come back after the War Dog. Whether they liked it or not, the gunman had a compulsion to kill Toby. Fair or not fair, the gunman had to be stopped before somebody else got hurt. After all that Bauer and Mags had gone through to try and save this War Dog, the last thing they wanted was for Toby to be killed now. Or ever.

The War Dog had done nothing to hurt anybody, and, considering the pain he'd been in, he was really easygoing. At this point, Bauer wouldn't put it past this gunman to have done something to make it jump or to fight back in order to have an excuse for killing it. Mags did say that Toby took a kick to the ribs. That would do it.

Also Bauer had asked Mags to get Sarah to go through the clinic's files and see if they could find the case of the dog that had been shot months earlier, supposedly by the neighbor. It was a wild guess, but that effort was ongoing, yet apparently not all that easy. Mags had records, of course, but, without a name to go on for either the patient or the human, Sarah had no way to search, other than manually. He'd asked Mags whether they'd contacted the cops at the time, and she just shook her head.

"You only call the cops if something happens to a human, at least in my experience. I'm under no obligation to let them know when a dog has been shot. In this case, the owner was here *supposedly*, and there didn't appear to be anything anybody could do about the dog."

"Right." Bauer scrubbed his face. "It was a long shot, and I really don't feel that the guy from two months ago would wait this long to retaliate. You might as well tell Sarah to stop her search."

Mags nodded and reached for the intercom button.

The rest of the day was spent wondering when they might get an update, plus when the next shoe would drop.

THE VERY NEXT morning, Bauer walked Mags and Toby down to the clinic and stayed with them, knowing in his gut that this gunman would be back. Bauer knew that waiting for the cops to solve this matter wouldn't help, so he and Badger and Mags had to come up with something themselves.

Once Sarah arrived, along with a cop with more questions, Bauer had quickly driven to Badger's and had picked up a few things. Badger's team had all kinds of stuff going on all the time, so they had a stockpile of goodies. Bauer grabbed some security cams and a whole security system to replace the unsuitable one she had at her home. This way, he could keep an eye on what was happening at the house. Still, if this gunman had skills, he could bust through even this advanced system pretty easily.

With the cameras set up outside and turned on, Bauer now sat with his laptop for most of the day. All through that remote surveillance, Toby stayed at his side, always wary. The War Dog never quite relaxed enough to sleep, even though Bauer had put a hand down to calm Toby several times.

When some people came in making noise, Toby became distressed, until he'd finally collapsed again, exhausted.

"It's all right, buddy, just rest," Bauer muttered.

At that, Sarah looked over at him. "Do you think it's all right though? This is the strangest scenario I've ever seen."

"You and me both," he agreed, with a nod. "Yet we have to trust that we're getting somewhere." She just gave him a flat stare. He returned the most confident smile he could manage, but, when she just snorted, he realized that he hadn't succeeded. She was a tough cookie. "You're sure you don't remember anything else about that previous case, *huh*?" he asked her.

She shook her head. "I have way too many patients coming and going on a regular basis," she snapped. "That isn't one that managed to remain in my head."

He didn't say anything else but wondered about her temper—but honestly the whole scenario was getting to everybody. He knew that it would be even harder on Mags, especially if there were any culpability on the part of her staff. He didn't even want to go there. But, as the day went by and then the next, with no solution in sight and no answers, he realized just how much damage just the stress of waiting was causing.

Something needed to break and soon. He just wanted it to happen in the right way. He was trying his best to keep people safe, and it was getting harder and harder to even keep them alert, as one day slipped into several more, and the people around him started to relax.

Even Toby seemed to relax slightly. "You've got to stay on your guard, buddy. This guy is out to get you." And, of course, that didn't help either because it just earned him still another glare from Sarah. "Sorry I'm in your hair so much," Bauer said.

She eyed him and then shrugged. "From the sounds of things, you'll be in my hair a whole lot more than I want anyway."

At that, his eyebrows shot up. "Meaning?"

"It's obvious you have a thing for her," she grumbled, looking anywhere but at him, "and surprisingly she seems to have a thing for you too. Here I thought you would be some short-term distraction, but you aren't, are you? That means you'll be around a bit more than I want."

"Why is it you think that's a bad thing?" Bauer asked. "I won't hurt her."

"You could hurt her without even being aware of it," she snapped, followed by a heavy sigh and another glare. "And I, for one, won't take kindly to that."

And then he realized what was the root of Sarah's attitude. It wasn't so much the whole gunman-dognapping scenario but the scenario with him and Mags. "I don't want to hurt her at all."

"Maybe not, but that doesn't mean that you'll avoid it. It's easy to hurt somebody and not even be aware that you're doing it."

"I'd like to think I'm aware enough that I would recognize if I was hurting Mags. In fact, I am certain I can manage that. And we're just at the exploring stage and haven't had much time, even for that."

Sarah shrugged. "So far, yeah, … but that won't last long. It's pretty easy to go from that to the 'let me betray you' and 'I didn't mean to hurt her' stage real fast."

At that precise moment, a phone call tabled the conversation, as she answered the call, relieved at the opportunity to cut him out of the conversation.

Still, Bauer found it interesting and wondered whether she had had such a bad experience herself that she was imprinting her negativity onto Mags or even keeping Mags's insecurities alive. Something to consider.

Later that evening, as he served up dinner to one very tired vet, he stated, "Sarah doesn't like me."

Mags looked up, laughed, and nodded. "Correction. Sarah doesn't like men."

He stopped, startled. "What?"

Mags nodded again. "She doesn't like men, … period. She has sworn off men permanently and, in fact, has a full-time relationship with a long-term female partner. I've known Sarah for a long time, and frankly she's much happier that way."

"Okay, that makes sense, I guess. I still wouldn't expect her to be quite so blatantly unhappy with my presence."

At that, Mags smiled. "You can't coax her around to your way of thinking," she replied, as she accepted the plate and sniffed the air appreciatively. "On the other hand, I can be bribed."

He burst out laughing. "One of the easiest bribes I've ever had to pay," he noted affectionately.

She looked over at him and smiled. "This whole cooking experience has been quite an unexpected bonus."

"Apparently, looking after starving veterinarians is a thing," he teased. "Who knew?"

"I certainly didn't," she murmured. "I thought I was doing quite well."

"Maybe you were," he stated. "I'm not sure how that works in your world. But seriously I was trying to talk to Sarah a little bit today, and she just wasn't having it. In fact, she called me out."

"Was she rude?" Mags asked in surprise.

"Not so much rude. More like warning me off. Telling me it was a short trip from being a nice guy to being an asshole, basically."

Mags gave a short nod. "Now *that* I can say is something she believes with every fiber of her being."

"Wow. I presume she's not like that with the patients."

"Hell no. That is not allowed," Mags declared. "It doesn't matter what the circumstance are, we have to treat all the patients nicely. And the owners of the patients too, I should say."

He nodded. "Good. I definitely got the impression that she wouldn't be at all disappointed if I were to disappear off the face of the Earth, preferably before I hurt you terribly, something she is certain I will do."

"Yeah, she's very protective. Don't take it personally."

"I didn't really take it personally. I was just trying to figure out what her underlying thinking was."

"She's been hurt, a lot," Mags shared. "Sarah's much happier in this relationship. Who knows? Maybe that's why she had to go through all she did, so she could find out where she really belongs. So, as long as you don't *hurt me*"—she made air quotes with her fingers—"she'll be fine. She'll adapt."

"I hope so," he murmured, "because I certainly didn't get that impression from her."

At that, Mags snorted. "Sarah is a person unto herself. She has been really good for the clinic, so I try not to do anything to upset that applecart." She looked over at him. "I would appreciate it if you didn't either."

"Wasn't planning on it," he stated, looking down at the clinic. "Hadn't realized just how much went into the day-to-day running of a place like yours."

"No, and that's one of the reasons I would be hard-pressed to replace her, if she got upset." At that, Mags sighed. "As a matter of fact, right now it would be a disaster, since we're already short-staffed. Although we have a couple new hopeful hires, who could help us a lot."

"Is my presence likely to do that?"

"I wouldn't have thought so," Mags noted, with a contemplative eye on him. "It's an interesting question though."

"It sure is from my perspective, because I don't want to cause you any trouble. I'm just not sure Sarah would be willing to let me stick around."

At that, Mags stared at him, startled. "Was it that bad?"

He nodded. "Yeah, I think so. Not on my side, but possibly on hers. Seems she approves of me for you as a distraction only, not anything more serious."

"Interesting. I'll have to see how she is and maybe have a talk with her."

"As long as it doesn't come across as me complaining," he added.

"No, that would be deadly. I'll see how it works out."

And, with that, he nodded and didn't say anything more.

"And we didn't get anywhere yet on the investigations, did we?" she asked.

"No, not as far as I had hoped. The only thing we found out was by cross-referencing the guy still in the hospital. Ken was in foster care for many years, so we're wondering if the other guy was somebody he met in the foster care system."

"I wonder if he goes to any group therapy or something like that," she suggested thoughtfully. "You know how that's another place for people to hook up."

"Sure, but the shooter and the intruder seem to be at opposite ends of the scales," he noted.

"Just because this guy is trying to kill dogs, ... I'm not sure that he hates dogs."

"Okay, now that is something you'll need to explain to me. How is it that it's not somebody who hates dogs?"

"I don't know how to explain it from his point of view," she admitted. "However, it just occurred to me that it's never quite so clear-cut. First, we can't think like him. Second, we project our own feelings and moralities onto others. Either way, we don't know what's going on in the shooter's mind."

He thought about her words long into the night, realizing that there were all kinds of scenarios where people had a love-hate relationship with animals. Sometimes they could see their way through it, and sometimes they couldn't. Bauer probably needed to check that out a little bit closer. Kudos to her for making him consider it because it was something that he hadn't even thought of.

He'd been going on the basis of somebody hating the animal, whereas it could be the opposite. It could be that he loved animals and had lost one, causing him to snap. Although that seemed completely foreign to Bauer. He wasn't sure there was any talking to those guys anyway. They got something in their head, and that was it. With that final thought, Bauer fell into an uneasy slumber.

When he woke up in the wee hours of the morning, he bolted to his feet. He wasn't sure what had woken him, but something was wrong. As soon as he stepped out of his bedroom, he heard Toby growling, low and deep. The War Dog stood in the hallway landing at the top of the stairs, staring down. Bauer placed a hand on his haunches, letting him know he was here. He whispered, "Just be quiet, buddy. Remember. We've got to be quiet."

Of course what Bauer really wanted was for this asshole to get inside the house, where Bauer could take him out—prepped and prepared this time, instead of having the shooter take off, after doing whatever the hell damage he thought he had the right to do. Still, the chances of the shooter taking off tonight without causing more trouble was pretty slim. At that precise moment, the bedroom door opened beside him, and Mags stepped out.

Taking one look, she whispered, "What is it?"

He held a finger to his lips, and she stepped up to his side and tried to peer down over the railing. Then they heard an ever-so-gentle step. She froze at Bauer's side, as he motioned for her to go into her bedroom and to call the cops.

She quickly nodded, looked down at the War Dog, then back at Bauer.

Bauer nodded. Toby was still not healed enough to go into a full-on fight. Even though the spirit was willing, the flesh was not. So, under duress, Toby was forced back into her bedroom. Afterward Bauer slipped quietly down the stairs. He'd only gone a couple steps when the back door slammed shut, and he heard the sound of someone taking off in the distance.

Bauer swore, as he raced out behind the intruder. He was less equipped for a dark run in the night, being more prepared for a battle in the house. As soon as he stepped out into the night, intent on pursuing this guy, bullets rang out against the side of the door. He ducked back inside, swearing again.

She called down from upstairs. "Are you hit?"

"No," he yelled back, swearing, "but it's almost like he baited me to come outside, then started firing."

"I wouldn't be at all surprised," she said, as she appeared beside him, her hands gently running over his face and shoulders. "Are you sure you're not hit?"

"I'm fine," he muttered, capturing her hands and tucking her up close, "but he's out there."

"You're not going outside," she stated firmly. "He has pinned us inside for a reason."

"Yeah, and that reason is what I need to figure out, so

stay here. Keep your head down, and let me do a quick check." And, with that, he bounded through the living room and the front entranceway. And then he saw it. Swearing, he picked up what seemed to be an incendiary device or a Molotov cocktail that hadn't quite started, then threw it outside. When it landed, it exploded into a small gush of flames.

She cried out beside him, "Oh my God! He wanted to burn us out or burn us down?"

"That was his plan, but it didn't go off."

"So, what do we have here, an amateur firebomber?" she cried out hysterically.

"Yeah, seems to be." And Bauer was even more concerned than before because this was another step further into violence, a step in the wrong direction from de-escalating. This guy was on a mission, and now his aggression appeared to not just be centered on the dog. Now it was directed at them, and that was not good.

CHAPTER 9

I T WAS HARD to imagine a rougher night than the rest of that one. Mags slept in fits and starts in the living room, while Bauer sat beside her, just a steady presence, that sense of security, so she could go back to sleep. Finally she muttered, "It's not that I'm upset."

"I know, but it just keeps going around and around in your head."

"It just blows me away that we've come to this," she murmured, "from nothing to this."

"I get it. I really do. Believe me. I would do an awful lot to keep you from this kind of a nightmare."

"It's not your fault," she murmured.

"No, it isn't, but I haven't managed to stop it either."

She realized he was taking this on as being his fault. As she snuggled against him, she realized she'd spent the bulk of the night curled up in his arms on the couch.

He asked her, "Do you think we've gotten past the point of going on a date yet?"

She snorted. "Very funny. I'm not even sure we've had a date."

"Oh, good. That means it's still out there ahead of us."

She rolled her eyes. "Always the comedian."

"I'm trying to be," he admitted, with a forced note of cheerfulness.

At that, she sat up and looked at him. "You don't have to always cheer me up. It's a nightmare, and I get that. But it's not your doing and I can't imagine going through it without you."

"It is a nightmare, but we are getting there." She shot him a look of disbelief, and he smiled. "I believe we are. It might not look like it just yet, but I'm a firm believer in positive thinking."

"*Right*," she muttered, as she sagged back.

He pulled her into his arms again and whispered, "Just relax. He won't come back tonight."

"What, because of the cops' presence? Jeez, it seems like they never left, and now they're back here again."

"Unfortunately the cops left long enough for him to show up."

"Right, so how does that work?" she muttered.

"Because he's watching," Bauer shared calmly. She shuddered at that. He held her close and whispered, "But so am I."

"And yet what would happen to anybody else in this situation? I mean, you happened to be available. I don't want to say you're out of work or anything, but you came because of the War Dog. What if I was alone, and this had happened?"

"Thankfully it didn't happen that way, and we're doing everything we can to ensure there's no repeat performance."

"I wish there was some guarantee," she whispered, "but I doubt that there is."

The cops came and talked to them several times, and she answered as best she could. Finally she admitted, "I might not even show up at the office tomorrow."

"News flash, tomorrow is Saturday."

She stared at him blankly. "Already? Wow."

"It is," he confirmed.

"Right, well, I still have office hours for a half day."

He groaned. "Oh, I was hoping you were closed tomorrow."

"I also have a second dog here too." She looked over to Millie, who was curled up beside Toby on the floor in front of them.

"Yeah, what's up with that? I thought Millie was just here for the one night."

Mags nodded. "True. But Millie's parents had a vacation scheduled and a pet sitter lined up, but their friend got ill. So we are serving as a temporary boarding house for Millie."

Toby was still on a leash, and so was Millie, so the cops could come and go as they needed to, without being disturbed by the dogs. Even at that, Mags sighed. "I need to hand this poor gal over, before she's any more traumatized."

"Millie? I think she's doing just fine." Bauer reached for her, petting her closest foot. Bauer got a lick for his efforts.

"Maybe, but I still won't be happy until I can get her handed off, without her getting antsy and nervous."

"Of course, and we'll do what we can to get that to happen on our end."

At that, the cops walked back in. "Okay, we're done for the night … again."

"Great, so what now? … You'll be back in another hour or so?" Mags asked the cop, clearly upset still.

"I hope not. We do have a team out looking through the woods for him." The cop studied her in the relative darkness of the living room. Bauer had insisted, hoping they would be less of a target that way.

"He won't be around now with the police still here," she muttered, with a wave of her hand. "You know that."

"We don't know it for sure, but I can understand why you would say that. We're definitely trying to do what we can to find him."

"What about a tracking dog?" Bauer asked.

She nodded at him. "Oh, that's a good idea." Then she looked back at the cop. "I mean, I don't know if this guy is around any longer or not, but it would certainly make me feel better to think that a tracking dog would be involved."

"We found no sign of his vehicle, so we presume he's long gone. And, no, that doesn't make us happy because obviously he's escalating."

At that, she didn't say anything, just stared at him. If there was ever an obvious comment, it was that, so it didn't deserve an answer.

The cop continued. "I'll be in touch."

As the officers took their leave, she turned to Bauer. "Great, so what does that mean?"

BAUER REPLIED, "MEANS he has to go process this stuff, write up a report, and probably get some sleep himself."

Mags groaned, shrugged ever-so-slightly, and declared, "If that's all then, I need to go back to bed."

He nodded. "Let's get you upstairs, so you can get a few hours of sleep. I promise I'll wake you up in time to go to the clinic."

She looked at the time. "Three in the morning. Wow. Another night shot." She yawned again, but he escorted her up the stairs to her room. She stopped at her door and looked back at him. "Do you think it's safe?"

"It's safe enough," he stated. "Go get some sleep." She stumbled into her room, closed the door, but then opened it almost immediately.

"Leave it open if you want," Badger suggested.

She frowned at him. "Will you hear anything down-stairs?"

"I will," he said. "Leave your bedroom door open, so the dogs can come and go as well."

"Right. I didn't even realize I'd left it open last night."

"It's good that you did," Bauer noted. "I think Toby heard the gunman first."

"Okay, so everybody's on duty, and I need some sleep." And, with that, she walked back into her room. Bauer returned to the living room, where he wrote up as much of a report as he could and fired it off to Badger. Though Badger was only a few minutes away, when it came to this kind of stuff, it was important to keep everybody in the loop. This way, Badger would see this message first thing in the morning, so he would at least start the day with an understanding of what the hell was going on here.

Now, if only Bauer did. He couldn't believe that the cops hadn't found this guy and that he'd shown up back here again, this time trying to burn down her place. As Bauer sat here in the darkness, leaning against the pillows on the couch, he realized that was probably not what the guy was trying to do. He probably was trying to chase them out of the house, so he could shoot the dog. Something to keep in mind for the next time. There was a really good chance a sniper situation was out there.

At that thought, something else occurred to Bauer, and he picked up his phone and started texting Badger again. Because a sniper meant one thing, and a good sniper meant military service of some kind. Now they just had to get him, before he had another chance to get them.

CHAPTER 10

MAGS DRAGGED HER sore body out of bed, right into a hot shower. As she stood under the waves of warm water crashing down on her, she realized just how much of a drain this was having on her too. She was exhausted, even without having done anything.

And yet that kind of thinking wouldn't get her anywhere. Pulling herself together, she quickly dressed and headed to the kitchen, already appreciating the fact that her houseguest was most likely up and ahead of her, which meant hot, fresh coffee when she hit the kitchen. She told him so, as soon as she walked in. "That's a huge benefit of having you here, you know. There's always coffee."

He looked up and grinned at her. "Good morning to you too. Sounds like you got some sleep."

She shook her head. "It's a lie. An absolute lie. I got no sleep. Some asshole was disturbing us, when I needed to be sleeping," she grumbled. She quickly downed her first cup of coffee, and, as she went to pour a second one, noted he was cooking. She sniffed the air. "You're making breakfast?"

"Sausage and eggs. Have a seat. It'll be ready in a minute."

She sat down, her stomach grumbling. "You know you don't have to look after me."

"I'm looking after myself," he said easily. "You just fit

into the same parameter quite nicely."

She snorted at that. "That almost makes me sound a bit *convenient.*"

"Oh, no, I'm not going in that direction. That's likely to get my ass kicked."

She chuckled. "It is nice to know we have a decent camaraderie, even when the chips are down."

He looked over at her and nodded quickly. "You know that's really important."

"Maybe," she muttered, wondering if she should have even brought it up. "It's just not exactly a realistic stage of life right now."

"The good news is, if you can get through something like this when it's really tough, everything else becomes that much easier."

She pondered that throughout the morning, as she worked quickly at the clinic, and, by noon, when the clinic was officially closed, and they had all the animals sent away, she looked down at Toby. "Hey, you ready to go home, buddy?"

He barked and wagged his tail. He was getting stronger day by day. She didn't have to help him in and out of the vehicle. He was jumping and running. Every once in a while, he would yelp because his leg was sore, and she had to restrict him when he wouldn't stop chewing at his stitches. Yet all of that was quite normal. As his stump healed, it itched, and nobody liked itching.

Along their way back up to the house, Bauer at her side, she broke the silence between them. "You're pretty quiet."

"Just got some information in, and we're trying to verify it."

Her ears picked up. "On our shooter?"

"Maybe. Last night it occurred to me that, if we had a sniper out there, chances are he was US military trained."

She winced. "Military?"

"Yeah, navy, air force, army. In theory it would be military of some sort, but sniper training under special circumstances can happen for many reasons."

"So what you're basically saying is this guy probably worked for and was trained by Uncle Sam."

"Yeah, that's what I'm saying," he confirmed.

"So, we're looking for a very angry sharpshooter who hates dogs?"

"It's possible, yes, but we don't have anything solid on that yet. I've got Badger looking into it too. I texted the detective and told him my theory, but, of course, I haven't heard anything back yet." Bauer gave her a wry smile.

"No, and you'll probably just get more pressure to stay out of their investigation."

"Pretty much," he agreed, with another grin.

"The thing is, if you stay out of the investigation, we will get our asses kicked. This gunman is still around. I don't know about you, but I feel like he's there each and every day."

"I wouldn't be at all surprised. I did put cameras in various places up in the woods, but we're too far away for a live feed, so I have them set up with SD cards."

She stopped and stared. "Really?"

He nodded. "What I need to do is go pull them, and I'll do it as soon we get some lunch."

"Or you can do it now," she suggested, "and I'll work on lunch while you're gone."

"I can do that," he agreed, but then he frowned. "I wondered about taking Toby with me."

She shook her head. "I wouldn't want to push his luck that far," she replied. "Another week, maybe two, and he'll be up for it, but right now? I would only recommend that kind of movement in an emergency, like if we had to make a run for it or something."

"Right, so in that case, it's just me out there."

At that, she grimaced. "Okay, now I feel bad."

He laughed. "Don't worry. You work on lunch, while I go switch out the cards. I got extras, so I can just swap them out. Then we'll have a look and see what's on them." At that, he walked through the house, made sure it was empty, and added, "I don't need to tell you to lock up, right?"

"I'm not sure what good it will do with a trained sniper and arsonist around, who has a key to my house, but okay," she grumbled in a hard tone. She followed Bauer to the door, then locked it behind him. Then she raced to the kitchen with Toby behind her and studied his progress. She looked down at the War Dog. "It's becoming quite a habit to have him around, isn't it, boy?"

Toby barked softly, as if he understood.

She smiled. "I'm not sure it's a *good* habit though," she admitted to him. "It's definitely the kind of thing I could get used to," she muttered to herself.

With a heavy sigh, she started looking for what options they had for lunch. She needed to do a major shopping trip. She always had a lot of dog food down at the clinic, so Toby's meals were taken care of, but in terms of theirs? Well, not so much. Bauer had been great with all the cooking, but, with two of them, they didn't have any leftovers, which is what she always relied on for weekends. However, in this current situation, it wouldn't work.

Bauer needed a lot more food than she did, and she had

certainly noticed he was more than ready to step up and to take care of things, even though she was a bit of a slacker in that regard. But then he wasn't dealing with clients and surgeries, and she was, so she would cut herself some slack over that whole deal. Besides, as long as he didn't feel put out, she would accept everything he did with gratitude.

God knows she needed a break from some of this work. And yet, as she stood here, watching his progress up the hill, she really hated to see him going out there alone. But, with the doors locked, with the new security in place that he'd mentioned in passing, she hoped they would be okay in Bauer's absence.

She pulled out fixings and managed to make up several sandwiches. She looked at the finished product, frowned, and made two more. She was hungry, and she knew he would be especially hungry after the walk he was on. She kept checking on his progress, but he would disappear into the trees, and then she'd see him come out again, only to disappear once more. The trouble was, if anybody else saw him, he could be a target himself, or they could take the opportunity to come down here, knowing that she was alone. Neither made her feel very good, particularly with Toby not quite back up to full strength.

But the War Dog was coming along and was so much better. Mags bent down and gave him cuddles. "We'll definitely talk to Badger about keeping you, if we can," she whispered, leaning over to give him a big hug. His tail was going like crazy, and she laughed. Just then a horrible thought occurred to her. What if one of these two men had the right to keep the War Dog?

It would just devastate her if she had to give Toby back to somebody who had been abusive. Yet the second man had obviously been trying to save Toby, and that was just as confusing. As she sat here, wondering what to do while she waited, she automatically put on a load of laundry. She switched out her bedding and then went to put on fresh coffee. When she put the wet laundry in the dryer, Bauer still wasn't back. Starting to get nervous, she looked out the window again, and, to her relief, she watched him slowly making his way toward her, but he was limping.

She hated that and studied him carefully to see how bad it was. It looked as though maybe he'd twisted his ankle or something, though of course her mind went to the worst-case scenarios, wondering if he'd been in a fight, had to dodge a bullet or some other godforsaken thing. She raced to the back door, and, as soon as he was close enough, she jerked it open. "What happened?"

He gave her a smile and shrugged. "It's all right. I just took a tumble down the hill."

She frowned at him, and he frowned right back. Then she laughed. "I'm glad to see your sense of humor hasn't been affected," she muttered.

"Nope, it's all good," he declared.

"Did you see anyone out there?"

He shook his head. "No, nothing."

"Oh."

He nodded. "I know. I'm of two minds myself. On the one hand, I kind of want to get shot at, so I can find out where this asshole is, but, then again, if he's a sniper and he's got good weapons, I'm in the worst possible scenario."

"We don't need any more injuries around here," she murmured.

"I get it," Bauer agreed, as he made it into the house and they quickly shut the door and locked it up.

She watched as he did something extra to the door. "Now what are you doing?"

"The locksmith still isn't coming for a couple days yet, which honestly really pisses me off, but I can just put this bar on." Then he showed her what he had done. "So if they get the lock open, they still have to get past the bar."

She nodded slowly. "Has this been on every night?"

"Since last night anyway."

"Good. I didn't even know about it."

"Sorry, I didn't think to tell you. I have one for the front door too. I was just trying to keep one more layer in place to slow down this guy."

"And that's really all anybody will do, isn't it?"

"If he's determined, he will find a way—until we stop him," Bauer stated. "That's the problem with these guys. If they're on a mission to get something or someone, it'll take an awful lot for anybody to stop them."

She stared at him. "We're talking about a bullet, aren't we?"

"He's coming at us with guns," Bauer pointed out. "It'll likely take a gun to take him out."

"Right." She considered it for a moment and then nodded. "I don't happen to have a weapon, you know."

"Yes, but thankfully I do."

"I know. Did you take it out there with you?"

He laughed, then pulled back his vest, and she saw the shoulder holster. "After the Molotov cocktail, I decided it was no longer optional and started wearing it all the time."

"That makes sense, though I suppose the cops won't be happy about it, will they?"

"It's not our job to make them happy. If they have a problem, then they better catch the gunman first," Bauer declared cheerfully. "Then it will no longer be an issue."

She laughed at that. "Somehow I still think it'll be an issue."

He shrugged. "Hey, I'm completely licensed, and the gun was legally purchased, so that's not my problem. Right now, the deal is keeping you and Toby safe, any way that I can."

"Thank you for adding me to that equation," she noted in a wry tone.

He just laughed, then motioned at her to go ahead of him. "Let's get to eating. I'm hoping you made lunch."

"Of course I did, but it's nothing fancy."

"Food doesn't have to be fancy to be good," he said, "but I definitely worked up an appetite."

"That's what I figured, so I just made lots of sandwiches. We really need to do some shopping."

"Sandwiches sound great." As they stepped into the kitchen, he sniffed appreciatively. "Not sure what you put in there, but it sure smells good."

"Fresh herbs," she replied, with a shrug, "to go with some of the fresh cheeses I had. So I did a selection." She motioned toward the platter on the table. "I also put on coffee, just to make sure I hadn't forgotten how."

At that he burst out laughing.

She grinned. "So, wash up, and we'll eat."

He headed off to the bathroom, washed up, and soon they were sitting down to a meal. Something she was very quickly becoming a little too comfortable with. Just that thought alone made her stop and consider the food in her hand.

"Something wrong?"

"I guess I was just realizing how comfortable we're becoming."

"I like it," he said. "It feels natural. It feels right." She looked up, startled. He nodded. "Doesn't it? Can you honestly say it doesn't?"

"I don't know. Maybe. I guess."

He smiled. "Do you know what it means to *damn with faint praise*?"

She chuckled. "I'm not trying to do that, but I'm also not trying to make this into more than it is."

"What is it?" he asked.

She raised both hands, shaking her head. "I'm not sure."

"Sure you are. It's called having a relationship."

She rolled her eyes. "Wow, that's really deep."

He grinned. "Is there any doubt that's what we're doing?"

"No, not really," she conceded, as she picked up a sandwich. "I just hadn't expected to get so comfortable, so fast."

"I like that you have," he admitted. "It makes me feel better." When she looked at him in surprise, he added, "I mean, think about it. You were pretty wary, but I guess you trust me now."

"I do trust you, and, yeah, you're right. That is a surprise." She frowned, taking a bite of her sandwich. "It's kind of a big one."

"I like it. I like it a lot."

"I get that, but then I'm just a little worried that I'm out here in left field, not really understanding what's happening."

"You understand exactly what's happening," he said, a twinkle in his eye. "And, if you would relax a little more, we could definitely take it a step further."

At that, she raised an eyebrow, then stared at him.

"Yeah, I know. I promised not to push." Then he laughed. "Apparently, when it comes to you, I have very little self-control."

She kind of liked that reply, and she could tell from his reaction that he had seen it too.

"See? You've come a long way." He chuckled, giving her a knowing look.

She shrugged. "I don't know about that, but it still feels as though there's a long way to go." And she meant it.

Just enough seriousness was in her tone that he understood that too. "No pressure," he reminded her gently. "Really."

"Says you," she muttered. "So, what's on the agenda for the rest of today?"

"I'm not sure. What do you need to get done?"

"I put laundry on because that needed to be done. My bedding is in the dryer because that was needed. I'm just thinking about all the other things that might need to get done today. I do have a bunch of bookkeeping to do that I normally do on weekends."

"You should definitely try to work that into your weekday routine," he suggested.

"I know I should, but it's never really been an issue before. There's a lot of stuff that I could probably shuffle around a little bit."

"You could also hire a bookkeeper."

"At the moment, when I'm still expanding and trying to do as much charity work as I can," she shared in exasperation, "paying somebody to do something I can do myself doesn't sit very well."

"Sure, but, then again, you're the most highly skilled person in the clinic, until you get a second veterinarian or even a partner there. Have you ever figured out your hourly rate, even just an average among all that you do there? Compare that to what a bookkeeper might charge you or a cleaning service or a groomer. Then you have a benchmark to help you decide. So, if that is something that somebody else can do—especially if cheaper than your going rate—then it frees you up to do more of the highly skilled work or makes time to focus on other aspects of the business."

She stared at him over her sandwich. "I never thought of it that way."

"I think we often forget that, if we aren't replaceable, we can't ever get promoted. I get that it's your own business, but, if you ever want to take time off, you also have to establish some boundaries so you can."

"That's another thing I hadn't gotten to," she admitted, "because it hasn't been an issue before."

"But now it is," he told her gently, "because we'll want to spend more time together."

"What if I want to work?"

"Then I'll deal with it," he said, with a shrug. "However, I suspect that, at some point in time, you'll want to have more time off."

She nodded. "It's been something I have started to think about, but, because I didn't really know what to do with my time off, it's been easier to just keep working."

"Got it." He chuckled, as he reached for part of the last sandwich. "Eat up," he said.

She shook her head. "Oh no, I'm done."

"Good. In that case, I'll be happy to take care of these," he noted, as he snagged both halves.

She laughed. "I forgot just how much food you can put away."

"Hey, I've seen some women eat some pretty hefty meals too."

"No, you're right. I've just never been much of an eater. Although, since you've come around, it seems like I'm doing a lot more of it."

"That's probably because you're always too tired to cook. And this week, you haven't gotten much of a chance to get a good night's sleep. So that definitely needs to be on the agenda, and we do need to go shopping too."

"Somewhere along the line, groceries need to be bought. I can order in a lot of stuff, and I do that more and more, as I try to preserve some of my own spare time."

"So, let's put in an order today," he suggested, "unless you want to do a trip into town."

She frowned at that. "I don't really want to leave the house."

"Why is that?"

"I just feel like this guy is out there, and our absence gives him a chance to get into the house again. I don't want to give him opportunities."

"I don't know if it makes you feel any better, but we have somebody else out there, keeping an eye on the place now."

She stared. "Seriously?"

He nodded. "Yeah. One of Badger's guys is out there. He's not very happy with something like this happening in their backyard, so they're all taking turns. It's a mix of his regular team, some part-time employees, and some volunteers."

She sat back and stared, looking stunned.

"No, they won't take your money. You're not paying them for their time," Bauer explained. "Believe me. They are very appreciative of all the times they've brought animals to you, and you've helped them out, so that's that."

She shrugged. "I guess that's what friends are for."

He smiled. "Exactly. They're just returning the favor."

It took her a minute, but she glared at him. "That was a cheap deal."

"I don't know about cheap, but it was necessary."

She continued to frown at him.

"Hey, I'll just frown right back at you," he said, "so you do you."

She sighed. "I'll thank Badger later."

"You do that. I'm sure he would appreciate it."

She nodded. "They're good people."

"Very good. And Kat does a ton of volunteer work for people who need prosthetics too."

She looked down at Toby. "I know. I was kind of wondering how she would feel about doing a dog prosthetic."

He frowned, then looked down at Toby and asked, "Do you think he'll need it?"

"No. Dogs can do well on three legs, once they are healed up and adjusted. But it would ease the wear and tear on the rest of his body that must adapt and work differently than it would have. In my opinion, it could give him a longer life, with less pain, and would reduce his fatigue."

"In that case, we can sure talk to her about it," Bauer said.

Mags shrugged. "It seems frivolous in a way."

"Toby is a retired War Dog. He has worked hard, and he deserves an easier life than he's had. I'm not worried about it being frivolous, and I highly doubt she would call it that either."

Mags laughed at that comment. "Okay, so when this is

over, maybe we can talk to Kat." She looked down at Toby. "Did you hear that, Toby? We might be able to get you another leg."

He just looked up at her and gave her a bark.

She smiled. "Considering that this guy is tired and needs some sleep, maybe an afternoon at home would suit us better."

"Agreed. So for the groceries, let's place an order. Other than that, let's just take care of things at home today. Besides, we can always call it a stay-at-home date."

She rolled her eyes at that. "Seriously? You're really trying to work a date into everything, aren't you?"

"I think I've done a pretty good job," he declared, with a big fat smile.

"You have, and it's kind of surprised me."

"What? That I've managed to work our date into so many conversations?"

"Maybe, and just the fact that I'm no longer quite so paranoid about it all. I thought you'd be the one who was paranoid."

"Me too, but somehow all of that changed when I saw you."

Something so quiet and so sincere about his tone had her turning, looking at him, wide-eyed. "Seriously?"

He nodded. "I didn't expect to feel this way, but honestly I think it's been building for quite a while. I just hadn't had the chance or the opportunity to spend time with you. You know? Just see what was there. So, in a way, I'm just as surprised as you are. Maybe I'd developed some habits too."

"You mean, that habit of keeping people out of our lives?"

He nodded. "Yeah, and it seems that we're both pretty

good at it. Or pretty bad, depending on your point of view."

"You're right, but then something like what we're dealing with right now kind of accelerates everything, doesn't it?"

"It sure does," he agreed, with a bright smile. "So once again, look at that. ... We're both on the same page."

She laughed. "You are nothing if not persistent."

"I am at that," he agreed, "but I'm also good people—and so are Badger and Kat and their entire team. I don't know if you trust them or not, but I sure do."

"That's who I called right from the beginning, so, yeah, I trust them. As much as I trust anybody, I mean."

"Well now, here's a twist. I'm pretty sure Badger sent me over here hoping that this would happen."

"Hoping what would happen?" she asked.

"That you and I would find something between us, enough to want to spend time together."

She stared at him. "What? Are you telling me that Badger and Kat were matchmaking?"

"I won't go so far as to say *that*." Bauer chuckled. "Maybe some *serious wishful thinking*."

She thought about it. "I can hardly argue about wishful thinking," she muttered. "I've done plenty of that myself."

He nodded. "You and me both. Besides, if it's true, then we owe them a *thank you*." She glared at him, after saying that. He frowned. "What? You can hardly argue that point."

"I can argue plenty of it."

"Just blowing smoke again," he said. "Smoke and mirrors, that's what you're doing."

She sighed. "Oh, please, I'll tell you what you can do with your smoke and mirrors, mister."

"Am I wrong?"

"Okay, fine. But we're not telling them anything, not

until we figure this out ourselves."

"No, absolutely not. We're not telling them until we figure it out, and that's final." He had to laugh. "I don't know about you, but I wouldn't have a clue what to tell them."

At that, she nodded. "Exactly. I'm still not sure what *it* even is."

"Do we have to label it or define it somehow?" he asked. "We want to spend time together, and we have done that quite nicely this last week. I don't really think we have to do more than that, except spend more time together and see where it goes."

"I mean, I know where I want it to go," she muttered, looking at him, "probably for the first time. I'm just not sure that I'm quite ready for it."

"No time like the present. If you feel like filling me in on where you want to go with this or to take this, I'm all ears."

She looked over at him and gave him a big fat smile. "It depends how you feel about exercise."

His eyebrows shot up. "Exercise?" he asked cautiously.

She nodded. "You know, like something to do this afternoon."

He slowly shook his head. "Okay, I'm dense apparently, so you'll have to be a whole lot more specific."

She burst out laughing. "Oh, I don't think so. Just because I haven't put a whole lot of trust and effort into long-term committed relationships, that doesn't mean I don't have some experience with shorter-term relationships." His eyes widened, and she went a bit red in the face. "Unless of course you're not interested."

He just stared at her, as if he didn't know what to say.

Then she started to laugh. "I'm not sure, but I think I might have surprised you for a change."

"If you're saying what I think you're saying, you definitely have, but believe me. I am more than up for the challenge."

She looked at him and smiled but cautioned him, "I don't necessarily want this to become something else."

"It already is something else," he declared. "So, if this is your way of making it just temporary, then the answer is no." He faced her, making sure she heard him and really saw him too. "I get that I was kind of pushing to get you to this point, but I really want more."

She sat back and stared. "Seriously?"

He nodded. "Yeah, seriously. I can't believe I'm saying this, but, if that's what you're looking for, I mean, any other time I would be more than happy to oblige. ... However, right now, I'm more interested in the whole enchilada."

She sat here, stunned.

He grinned, then got up and leaned over and kissed her hard. "Coffee?"

BAUER COULDN'T BELIEVE he'd refused her offer, but that was truthfully what he wanted. He didn't want Mags to treat this as a casual relationship, an affair to be tossed off afterward. He wanted her to take it seriously. He wanted her to take them seriously. She'd come a long way, but it was not hard to see that she was comfortable with an affair, yet not comfortable with a commitment. He understood it because he'd been there himself.

At the same time, that wasn't where he wanted to be

anymore. Not with her. He knew the shrinks would have a heyday, if he ever sat down and tried to discuss it, but it was true, and he was fighting not only for himself but for them. For what they could be together. That alone made it completely worthwhile.

As the afternoon wore on, she slowly relaxed again, and he could see her letting go of some of the tension. She was relaxed, and some of that wariness in her eyes had eased back, but he still caught her looking at him sideways, as if trying to figure him out.

"I knew it wouldn't be that easy."

"Yes, and I meant it." She glared at him, but he shrugged. "Hey, you're worth it." Her eyebrows shot up. "*We're* worth it," he clarified. "You just need to trust a little bit more."

She shook her head. "This is just a game to you."

"No way, no games," he declared. "When I want something, I go after it. Is that wrong? I don't think so. I think it's very important that we know exactly where we stand with each other."

"I don't have a clue where I stand with you," she replied.

He looked over at her and gave her the tenderest smile he could manage. "*Yes*, you absolutely do. You just don't know what to do with it." With that, he added, "Listen. I'll sit down and go over some of this information that I've gotten from Badger and see if I can come up with something to go with from here. This waiting around is very irritating."

"Ya think?" she quipped, with half a snort.

Then she groaned, as he laughed at her. "It'll be fine," he said.

"I'm glad you think so," she muttered. Then she got up and switched over the laundry, while he kept half an eye on her. When she was done with that, she sat down, still restless.

"You seem to need something to take your mind off all that's going on."

She glared at him. "I thought I had a good idea earlier."

He flashed a brilliant grin. "Yep, you sure did," he agreed. "I just need it to come with a little more than a five-minute quick-and-easy roll in the hay."

"You're that fast?" she asked, almost in a mocking tone.

"Hey, I can be as fast or as slow as you want," he stated. "I just want the end result to be the same."

And, with that, she glared at him and flounced off to her bedroom.

He slowly closed his eyes and sent up a silent prayer to whoever might be listening because, man, oh man, he would need all the help he could get. There was nothing he wanted more than to join her on that huge bed of hers and spend an afternoon enjoying just being together.

A part of him was torn; another part of him understood that it would only be the right thing to do if he wanted something short-term. But he didn't, and the longer he was with her, the more he realized just how much she meant to him and how much he really did want the whole enchilada. He couldn't let her toss this off as a casual affair just because she was afraid. He could see that, in her mind, it was an acceptable alternative right now.

Still, he wanted more, and a temporary fling wasn't worth walking away from a chance at something that could be so much better. He just needed to convince her that this was what she wanted too. He could see her wondering about it, contemplating the process in her mind, trying to figure out what to do and how to take his counteroffer.

He didn't want to be too difficult or to make things too

complicated. He didn't want her to get confused and be upset about it, but he certainly didn't want her to think of him as a casual affair either. He was more than happy to have an afternoon of fun with her, but he didn't want that to be all it was.

As he dialed Badger, he thought about how strange and crazy his world had become. "Hey, you got any news on who this gunman might be?"

"No, not yet," Badger said. "I'm getting stonewalled. It's getting much harder to find somebody these days for some reason."

"We're looking for anybody who was medically discharged or discharged for poor conduct. Anything along those lines, particularly somebody with canine experience."

"You think he was a handler?" Badger asked in shock.

"I'm not sure what I think at this point. I'm not sure if he was a handler himself or if he was connected to somebody who might have been a handler. What I can tell you for certain is that he feels very strongly that this War Dog doesn't have the right to live, and he'll take extreme measures to make sure he doesn't live much longer."

"Which is fascinating in itself," Badger murmured, "but it's just not helpful in trying to track down this asshole."

"What about the cops' investigation to date, and what about the one guy in the hospital?"

"Yeah, so again we have a name. *Ken.* I do have some history on him now. He was military, and he got badly injured when an IED blew up on the roadside," Badger shared.

"Any connection to dogs?"

"No."

"What about his known friends and family?"

"Family, no. Foster care, yes. We're working on military friends who may have been discharged around the same time. The other thing would be anybody who might have been in the foster family with him."

"Right. Anything on Ken's childlike innocent way of speaking?"

"Apparently the medication he's on is partly responsible, and it's partly because there was brain damage from the IED. He lives in a halfway house close by."

"So, send me the address for that, and I'll go talk to them."

"I was just sending it, right when you called."

"Good. I could use a chance to get out of here."

At that, Badger's tone turned curious. "You two not getting along?"

"We're fine," Bauer muttered.

"I figured you would be," Badger answered slowly. "I hope she's not feeling too stressed by having you there."

"I don't know," he replied, with half a laugh. "Things get a little confusing sometimes."

"I'm sure they do, but you're a smart man. You'll figure it out."

After a moment of silence, Bauer chuckled. "It keeps things interesting. I have a suspicion you tried to set me up," he stated, a note of accusation in his voice.

"Yeah, so does that mean you'll get mad at me or thank me later?"

"Depends on how it all works out," Bauer declared, with a hard note. "At the moment it looks like I'll have to kick your ass across town and back."

At that, Badger burst out laughing. "You and what army?" he jeered, but still with a happy tone. "You know that it would be a hell of a thing if it worked out."

"It would be," Bauer agreed, "but, in the meantime, it seriously sucks."

"I know, man, but nothing easy ever made a good life. Some things you have to work at in order to make it worthwhile," Badger suggested.

"It would also be nice, every once in a while, if something would work out without being a pain in the ass, you know?"

"She's good people."

"Yeah, she is. Doesn't mean it'll be easy. She's got some issues."

"So do you," Badger replied. "Break through together and you'll both be happy."

"It takes two," Bauer mumbled, and a moment of silence came on the other end.

"Ah, well, I don't know what the problem is, but we're rooting for you."

"That's not helping," he barked.

"Maybe not, but I suggest you go to that halfway house. I've got a couple guys taking over shifts watching the house. One of them is up in the woods, and the other is down closer, so she should be safe for a few hours."

"Okay. I could use the break. Speaking of breaks, Mags mentioned something about a prosthetic for Toby. It would be huge if you could talk to Kat about it." And, with that, Bauer signed off and ended the call.

When he turned, he found her standing there, her hands on her hips.

"Now what?" she asked.

"I have the address for the halfway house where the other guy came from, the one in the hospital, *Ken*," he explained. "Badger told me how that guy was injured in an IED blast and is on medication. We've now got a case of a brain-damaged guy, and he must have emotional issues as well. I don't even know quite what to call it."

"It's obvious from the way he spoke that he's regressed in some ways," she noted.

He nodded. "He loves animals."

"So, what is it you're hoping to find when you go there?" she asked curiously, as she walked into the room.

"I'm hoping to find his buddy, the shooter and would-be arsonist."

At that, she stopped. "You think they're friends?"

Bauer nodded. "I think they at least know each other. It's hard for me to think that these are two completely separate and isolated incidents. Whether they heard about the dog at the same time and went in different directions, I don't know. Badger's checking through our hospital guy's military records for anybody who came to visit him while he was in the military hospital, and I'll head up to the halfway house where he lives and see if I can come up with something there." She frowned, as he added, "I know it's not what you want to hear, but two men are watching the place." She frowned at him, and he nodded. "Badger's men. Remember?"

She sighed. "He's saying it's safe?"

"Yes, he thinks it's safe for me to go out. I need to check out this lead, especially since it's all we have at the moment."

"Fine. ... I'm not sure I agree, but I can see that it's something you want to do."

"It's something I need to do," he said. "And, to tell you the truth, getting out for a little bit wouldn't hurt either."

Her eyebrows shot up. "Right," she replied, her voice a

little distant. "A little space would be nice." At that, she turned and walked back upstairs into her bedroom, almost slamming the door closed.

He winced at that turn of events, but, putting that personal conflict on hold, he got up, packed his phone, grabbed a water bottle, and called out, "I'll keep you posted." With that, he disappeared out the door and headed for his vehicle.

As he drove down the long driveway, he looked back to confirm everything looked normal. It was just one of those habits. He hated to leave her, but, at the same time, he knew that, as long as she was safe and under watch, a bit of a break would be helpful. He couldn't believe he was doing what he was doing, but, in his heart of hearts, he also knew it was the right decision.

He didn't want just a little time with her. He wanted a long time. The time of their lives.

CHAPTER 11

MAGS WATCHED BAUER drive away, feeling the ache of the loss already in her heart. He would only be gone for a little bit, but it seemed so much longer, so much worse. She shook her head. "You're being an idiot." But what was she supposed to do? She'd blocked off her heart a long time ago, and now he was prying it open, one step at a time.

Although she'd had rejection before in her life, it hadn't been something she'd expected in this instance. While she understood his reasoning, it made her furious, angry, and manipulated. Yet, at the same time, she couldn't do anything but admit that it was a hell of a thing. He wanted everything and was willing to sacrifice short-term gratification, holding out for more, … for all of it. The *whole enchilada*, he had said. And was there any reason not to go along with that?

Dammit, she really liked the man. She more than liked him, to be honest. Something was so very addictive about his personality. About who he was and the way he acted on a day-to-day basis. He was fun to be around. He was good company, and he made her feel safe, and that feeling of safety was part of the problem. She didn't necessarily want some-one to make her feel safe, yet at the same time she was terrified that, if she felt safe, but then it all blew to hell, she would suffer all the more once she was alone again.

Of course, just because she might suffer didn't mean she

would suffer long and hard or that it would be the same scenario as last time. She was literally being a chicken-shit about the whole thing. That just made her feel even worse. That and the fact that she'd let him take off without any kind of a goodbye, without any kind of warning to look after himself, and that just made her feel worse.

She stared down at her phone, not knowing what to say at this point in time. She was trying to figure out if contacting him now would get her even further into trouble, but, in the end, she couldn't help it. She quickly texted and stared down at the message she had written. **Stay safe.** Then she hit Send. Surely it was innocuous enough that he wouldn't take it the wrong way. When she got a response not very many minutes later, she stared at it and groaned—but couldn't stop smiling.

I love you too.

She sighed. "Now, if only that were true," she grumbled.

At that, she brought herself up short. Was that the problem? Was it just that she didn't think he loved her enough? Because he seemed to be shooting that down pretty fast. She didn't even know that love had anything to do with this, but isn't that what she was looking for? Wasn't that the promise? The holy grail that she thought she needed in order to have a relationship again? Because that was foolish. It was beyond foolish and, in many ways, just plain stupid. And nobody would have ever said that she was stupid.

Yet here she was, acting like a two-year-old, wanting everything. At that, she stopped, realizing that's exactly what he'd said. He wanted *everything*, and he didn't want just a roll in bed for the afternoon. He wanted something serious, solid, and enduring.

She slowly sank to the side of her bed. "Damn it."

She had no choice but to admit it. That was precisely what she wanted too. Now the question was, what would she do about it? Just then Kat called. Mags stared down at the phone for a moment, before she answered. "Hey, Kat. What's up?"

"Earlier, when Bauer was talking to Badger, I heard mention of maybe doing a prosthetic for Toby," she began. "I don't have any real experience in that area—although I have already been designing some for various animals—but I'm willing to give it a try if you are."

Mags brightened. Of course she took another pang to her heart as she realized that this was Bauer's doing. Setting this up for the War Dog, a dog he barely knew but already cared about. "If you could, that would be fabulous."

"I know it's not a good time in terms of bringing Toby here," she noted. "I wondered about a future date coming up though."

"Oh, sure." Mags hesitated. "Although I'm honestly not sure that the timing is all that good just now for Toby."

"No, you're right," Kat noted. "I would need him completely healed, with no swelling at the stump, to really see what will work best for him. How close is he to that?"

"Not that close yet," Mags admitted. "Look. Why don't we push it off a week or even two. Hopefully this whole situation will be in a much better place by then too."

"How is it going?" Kat asked, a curious tone in her voice. "I hope it was okay that we sent Bauer up there to you. He was essentially there to look after the War Dog, but I understand he stayed to look after you."

"Yeah, and that's a weird feeling in itself," she admitted honestly. "You know when you've been independent for a long time, it's kind of a strange scenario when somebody else is stepping up to help you, even though you didn't realize that you even needed the help."

Kat noted, "We've known each other for a long time, Mags, so I hope I can speak freely. I can tell you right now that there are times in everybody's life when you don't know what you need. Sometimes life just hits you, and you just need to let things happen. Sometimes you need to get out of your own way and let things roll in the direction that's best for everyone," Kat suggested. "In this case, I guess Badger and Bauer and the cops are all starting to pick up a few leads to work, so maybe some things are starting to happen. I can see that it may not be the most comfortable place to be in right now, but Bauer is a good guy, and he really knows what he's doing."

"I hope so," Mags said, with half a laugh, "because I've already let him in. So, if he's no-good, I'll be a little late in shutting the proverbial barn door." At that, Kat's gentle voice mentioned something Mags would always remember.

"Sounds to me like you let him in a little more than you thought you would."

Mags stopped and pinched the bridge of her nose. She was at a loss for words, feeling the tears come up at the corner of her eyes. "You can sense that already, *huh*? And here I thought I was hiding it so well."

"Not from me," Kat said. "All I can tell you is that he really is a good man. If you guys could make something work, I think it would be a hell of a dynamic, but only if that is what you want. No pressure, … particularly from Bauer, I'm sure. He's just not that kind of guy."

"He seems to be very …" Mags hesitated. "I want to say *patient*, but maybe *understanding* is a better word."

"*Understanding* is good," Kat said. "He's been around,

working with us off and on a lot for the last few months. I know that he worked with Badger years ago in the navy, so I can tell you that Bauer's honorable, solid, and a good man to have on your side, especially when things go south."

"That's definitely been proven out," Mags muttered, staring around her. "I just can't believe I'm even in this situation."

"No, and I'm so sorry. If I had realized the War Dog would cause you this kind of trouble, we would have sent somebody over and tried to find another answer."

"Well, you *did* send somebody over," she stated, with a chuckle. "I just didn't realize that particular somebody would put me in such an interesting spot."

"You are only in whatever spot you want to be in," Kat stated firmly. "Now, if your heart is affected, then talk to him about it. If it isn't, then let yourself off the hook and don't feel like you owe him anything. That's not why he's there."

"No, I know that," Mags said, "but what if I'm on the hook, and he's not?"

"Then you're not talking to each other, and maybe you should be."

"What do you mean?"

"Bauer doesn't do easy and light. He got badly hurt a long time ago, and, for him, a commitment is a commitment and not something he would ever make lightly. Add to that the whole injury and the perception by some that anyone with such an injury is somehow less than whole. That's a bigger deal than you may realize for him. I suspect that he's at a point in his life where he's looking for something long-term or not at all. If he wanted to keep his life simple and do the one-night-stands thing, he would have done it already, but he hasn't. He's very much a long-term kind of person, but, if you're not looking for that, then it's fine. Just tell him," she said easily. "You guys can work this out. It's not that big a deal." And, with that, Kat rang off.

Mags stared down at the phone. "Well, Kat, you're right about some of it and very wrong about the rest," she muttered. "It's a very big deal, and I don't know that it will be all that easy to work out." But, in her heart of hearts, she realized the problem was her because she definitely wanted Bauer, of that she had no doubt.

The other problem was, did she want to commit to a long-term relationship? The fact that apparently everybody in his world knew that he was a long-term guy also surprised her. It meant that he didn't have a lot of girlfriends or affairs and didn't get into relationships easily.

Of course nobody knew how their relationships would end up, but, if you went in with the intention that it would be good, could you ask anything more of somebody? And, if that's what he was looking for, what the hell had she been looking for? Because she didn't just want an afternoon in bed either. She really liked the man.

She wanted him—a hell of a lot more than just an afternoon fling. It was that fear factor again.

Shaking her head, she busied herself doing chores, until hours later, when she realized there was still no sign of him. She quickly texted him. **How much longer?**

He sent back a question mark, adding, **Not sure. Why?**

She searched for a plausible answer to that, and then her gaze landed on the kitchen. **Dinner.**

I can pick something up, he suggested.

She thought about it, then shrugged. **Sure. Why not?**

His next text read, **Enjoy your afternoon. Just take it**

easy and relax, if you can.

With that text, she realized, even while he was out doing what he was doing, still her care and her concerns were on Bauer's mind. He was a hell of a good man. So, what the hell was her problem? On that note, she headed up to her bedroom and to the journal that she used to write in all the time.

Turning back the pages, she took a look at all the old notes she had written about her breakup, including the promises she had made to herself to never get hurt quite so badly ever again. She realized just how foolish it all was. If she didn't put herself out there, sure, she would never get hurt, but she also wouldn't experience some good things in life either. In fact, she could hurt herself by not allowing love to come into her life.

By doing what she had done, she'd locked herself into the same empty, lonely place. She needed to ask herself some hard questions. Did she want to be in that place, or did she want more for herself? She had buried herself in more work, in the struggle of running her own business, but it didn't have to stay that way. She could have so much more in her life, and one of them was right there for the taking.

All she had to do was reach out and accept him and his offer.

BAUER RETURNED TO the halfway house that he'd been at earlier, but that first visit had been during lunchtime. The woman he'd spoken to told him that he'd have better luck talking to somebody more knowledgeable if he came back after lunch. This woman was a new hire, and the regular staff would be coming in around one o'clock.

He checked his watch, noting the staff should have had time to get in and to get situated for the day, so that he could at least maybe get some answers this time.

As he walked up to the front door and stepped into the residence, some guys stepped out, laughing and joking with each other. He didn't know where they were going, but wherever it was, it was all in good fun. He smiled, and, with that smile still on his face, he turned to see a woman studying him.

"Are you the guy who came earlier?" she asked.

"I am." He gave her a quick nod. "I'm looking for any information you had on Ken's family."

"Ken is in the hospital," she replied.

"I know. I'm trying to help the veterinarian who was looking after the dog to see if we can find out who else in Ken's world might have some answers for us."

She shrugged. "I don't even know that I'm allowed to talk to you."

"Have the police been here?"

She nodded. "They have, yes."

"Did they ask about any of his known associates?"

She nodded. "Yes, so, if you have been talking to them, you should be able to get the information from them," she said shrewdly.

"I could," he conceded, "but I'm also looking out for the well-being of the dog. Therefore, we're trying to find out if Ken or his friends have any claims on the dog."

She frowned, her eyebrows almost coming together. "Ken is definitely not allowed to have pets here," she noted. "I don't know how he even heard about the dog."

"That was another question I would ask. Was there anybody talking about a War Dog? Was anybody talking about anything like that here?"

She shook her head. "Not that I know of, but I don't exactly monitor their conversations either," she stated. "Although Ken, for all his disability, is very intelligent. Every once in a while, he goes into this military mode. It almost seems to be play-acting, as if it's coming from his memory, from his experience. To me, maybe he's trying to save things. He has brought in squirrels that have been hurt. He brought in a cat injured in a vehicle accident one time. Anytime that he knew about something that needed some love, care, and attention, he tries to help."

"Presumably that's who he was before the accident?"

She nodded. "That would be my take on it," she replied. "I don't have any of his medical records though."

"That's fine. I can get all that from the police."

"So why can't you get this information?"

"I could, but I highly doubt that they asked the same questions that I need to ask," he explained, with a bright smile. "Believe me. I'm very concerned about the War Dog and the vet clinic that's been under attack over it."

"I don't understand any of that," she said, with a frown. "I can't see Ken ever hurting anybody."

"No, and I'm really hoping you're right. At the moment, it looks like he's been heavily involved in trying to rescue this dog."

"Of course," she agreed. "That would be something he would do. I have no doubt about that."

"But he couldn't have done it alone," Bauer noted. "He doesn't drive, does he?"

"No, no, of course not," she confirmed, then she realized where he was going. "However, he does get day passes to go out. He can go out with his friends, as long as they're on the approved list."

"Can I please see that approved list?"

She hesitated.

"I know you're wondering if it's even legal, so I'll make it easy for you. You can send the information to the cops."

"You don't mind?"

"No, not at all," he said. "I know it probably sounds bizarre, but we are working together."

She hesitated, then added, "I should phone them."

"Then do so," he replied. When she looked at him hesitantly, he added, "If you need to go into your office or whatever, feel free to do so and talk to the detective."

"What if he says no?"

"Then I'll call him and tell him to get his ass over here and to get the information himself, though he doesn't have any more time than the rest of the people in the world."

She winced at that. "It does seem like we're always so short-staffed, and I know for a fact that the police aren't any different."

"No, they sure aren't. Yet I don't want you to get in any trouble, so go ahead and call him."

She nodded. "I'll be back in a minute." And, with that, she quickly disappeared.

As Bauer looked around, he found one of the cooks looking at him. He smiled at her. "Don't suppose you know anything about who Ken hangs around with and who drives him around?"

She nodded. "I do, but I can't say that he's anything like Ken at all."

"In what way?"

"They were buddies in the war," she replied, looking

around nervously. "You know the kind, who are still bitter, still angry. Not like Ken, though obviously the accident changed him, but Ken had a big heart beforehand, and you can see that still. He didn't lose that, but this guy? ... I don't think he ever had a heart."

"Does he have a hatred of dogs, just opposite of the way that Ken loves them?"

Her eyes widened. "Oh, yeah," she confirmed. "Anything that is injured or hurt, Ken won't tolerate at all. However, his friend hates to even talk about sickness. Even when Ken has to take his medicine, this other guy gets grossed out, like upset and angry about the whole thing. We often have to tell him to leave until it's a done deal because Ken can get quite belligerent because that guy's here, starting a ruckus too. When that guy isn't here, Ken is quite decent about taking his medications."

"Right, but this buddy, he doesn't believe in what Ken's doing here then. In other words, he's doing a whole sham thing about being his friend?"

"Maybe, but I don't really know. We see all kinds of behaviors influenced by other people, and, just like children, they act out sometimes, and that is definitely the case with Ken and his buddy."

"Do you know this guy's name?" he asked.

She thought about it. "Glenn. I think it's Glenn, but I don't know his last name."

He nodded. "That's a start anyway. I don't know if I can get his name from anybody."

"You could ask at the hospital maybe."

"They are still struggling to get Ken's medication stable, so they won't let me in to see him. As a matter of fact, nobody's allowed in, not until the doctors clear it."

"Ken is special. I would be more than happy to keep him here any day. He's easy to get along with and full of heart. It is obvious to see that, even before, he was a good man. But this other one, not so much. I wouldn't be unhappy at all if that one never came back again."

At that, they heard footsteps, and the cook returned to her work. Bauer turned to look at the woman he'd spoken to earlier, who frowned and explained, "The detective asked me for the list and said to tell you to call him, and he would provide it for you."

"That sounds good," Bauer replied. "If you think of anything else along this line, please let him know."

She nodded, relieved that he wouldn't hassle her over it. With that, he waved his goodbye and walked out. As soon as he got to the car, he phoned the cop.

"What the hell are you doing, Bauer?"

"A job you guys should be out here doing. I get that you don't have enough time and resources and all that, but we have a woman here, a victim of a series of escalating crimes against her home and business and her life. She can't sleep because she's already had somebody breaking into her home, trying to burn down her residence, and shooting at her. So, if I'm out here doing some of the legwork that you can't possibly do, don't go getting in a snit about it."

"I can't just give you these names."

"The only one I'm interested in is Glenn."

"Why Glenn?"

"Because, while the administrator was talking to you, I was talking to the cook, and apparently Glenn has quite a negative influence on Ken's behavior. Glenn's got an attitude. He hates all animals, but what really sticks out is that Glenn hates dogs." At that, he heard the shuffling of paperwork from the cop's end of the call.

"Ken Hedrun, he's a veteran."

"Yeah, I suspected as much."

"Glenn's a buddy of Ken's from the military. They were both foot soldiers. I don't have a military record here though."

"But they were both in the same unit?"

He flipped through what he had and said, "It doesn't say much here. All it tells me is that he was a veteran too. He's been out about two years, and he's good friends with Ken, according to the halfway house records."

"Yeah, that's what I got as well. Do you have an address?"

"We'll go and check out the address."

"Good," Bauer noted. "Any chance you can send that information on to Badger?"

"I can, but what good will that do?"

"He can get more military background on him."

"In that case, I'm on it," the cop stated, and he quickly ended the call.

Bauer started his engine and looked around, with that weird sense of knowing. He couldn't see anything, but it was almost as if he knew the Glenn guy was out there, watching him. Almost in acknowledgment, he lifted a hand and waved and drove off. As soon as he got closer to another area of town, he phoned Mags. "What do you want me to pick up for dinner?"

"Did you find out anything?" she asked, forgetting about dinner and going straight to the heart of the matter.

"Yes. I've already connected with Badger and the cops. We've got a name and an idea of who the attacker might be. But first things first, we also need some food."

"Right. I guess I don't care then, whatever you like."

"Great. Burgers or Chinese?"

She laughed. "I figured you would say pizza."

"*Nah*, you seem like more of a Chinese food fan to me."

"I love Chinese," she shared.

"Fine, any places close by that you like?"

"I do know of one, but I haven't really tried all that many."

"I have a place in mind. I'll be there in about"—he looked at his phone—"give me say twenty, twenty-five minutes."

"Fine."

Yet Bauer detected an odd note in her tone. "What's the matter? Miss me much?"

She snorted. "Like a toothache." And, with that, she hung up.

He grinned. "That is progress."

CHAPTER 12

MAGS WAITED ANXIOUSLY, after talking to Bauer. For whatever reason, she felt her stress levels increase by the minute. Finally she texted him. **Something's wrong.**

Instead of texting back, he phoned her. "I'm ten minutes out. What's wrong?"

"I don't know," she admitted, getting up and pacing the living room, the phone in her hand. "It just feels wrong."

"Wrong how? Can you expand that a little more?"

"No, I can't," she snapped. "Just get home."

"I'm coming as fast as I can. The doors are locked, right?"

"Yes. And I've got Toby here, and he's not showing any signs of being bothered, so maybe it's just me."

"Doesn't matter if it's just you," he replied. "That's not the issue right now. If you're feeling something is very wrong, then we'll honor that."

"It just seems like you've been gone a long time. I haven't been ... Honestly I haven't been ..."

"I've got the food, and I'm almost there."

"Good," she said. "Hurry." And, with that, she disconnected.

She resumed her pacing, and, in a fit of urgency, she went up and down the stairs, until she realized that she was wearing Toby out and hurting him with too much movement.

"I'm so sorry, buddy," she said, finally sitting down on the living room floor. Toby came over, hobbling carefully in and collapsed down beside her. "Yeah, I should have just ignored everything else and looked after you instead," she muttered.

She gently checked on his bruising and the incision, which was good. "You're looking so much better. I want to ensure that you stay healthy."

Finding nothing else to do, she looked at him. "You've been through way too much to have anything happen to you now." And even that thought sent her into a tailspin again. She bolted to her feet, and instead of going up and down the stairs, she just paced around in circles.

Finally, tired and feeling like an idiot, she ended up crashing down beside Toby again, wrapping her arms around him, rocking him gently back and forth.

He snuggled in deeper, and she whispered, "I don't want to let you go." Animals had always had the ability to break her heart. She carefully avoided adopting every single one she saw. As she sat here thinking about it, she realized she could be bringing a lot of them home, then move them out to foster homes and people who would look after them. Just like Bauer had suggested. Just as she had done so long ago.

But somewhere around the time that she'd been left at the altar by her fiancé, she had stopped letting animals into her heart and home, as well. She realized just how much she had locked herself down, how much she had refused to allow herself to feel, just to avoid getting hurt. That meant an awful lot of animals that she probably could have helped along the way that hadn't gotten that help because she hadn't been capable, all because of fear.

"That's got to change," she declared to Toby, "because you need help, and a lot of other animals like you need help. Maybe we could set up some kind of training facility or just a rescue. I've got acres and acres here, after all," she murmured. "I need to go back to doing what makes my heart happy." She realized that was the difference. She had told herself she was happy all these years, burying herself in work and pretending to be happy, but she'd really just been existing, focused on growing her business. Yet happiness had never really entered into it. Until now.

"And I guess we're going to blame the big goof for that too," she muttered, with half a smile. The big goof of course being Bauer. He'd opened her heart just enough for her to see the light out there. As soon as she saw that light, she had tried to shut down things, but Toby here had gotten past her defenses. Then Bauer. Plus she knew she was no longer capable of shutting it down, as she had before.

She'd been very protective. Protective of her own space, her own peace of mind, and her heart. She needed to, back then, she realized, while she healed from the initial betrayal, which had then eked into her professional life. It wasn't that it was wrong. Mags had to do it to a degree because of the work she was doing, but she could afford to open up a little bit more now.

She could afford to be kinder, gentler, and maybe have somebody else in her life again. As she sat here, hugging Toby, she wondered what life with Bauer would mean. He would probably go off and do jobs like he was doing here for her but maybe not. Maybe he had plans for something much closer to his heart, more locally based. She hadn't even asked him about it.

She'd been so determined to keep him at arm's length

that she didn't want to know. She hadn't dared to dream. But now she was dying of curiosity, and she couldn't wait for him to get back. When she heard a vehicle pull up, she bolted to her feet and raced to look out the window. It was him.

She looked down to see Toby struggling to get to his feet. "Hey, buddy. I know it's hard on you, isn't it? I'm sorry that you feel you must get up every time we do."

She waited for Bauer to reach the front door, and, with Toby at her side, she unlocked it, pulling it open, with a bright smile on her face. "Glad you're here. I'm starving."

He nodded, but the look on his face wasn't normal. And his hands were up, and a man held a gun at his back. "Meet Ken's friend, Glenn," Bauer said.

Mags glared at the gunman. "*You*," she snapped in a snarling voice. "This is the guy who came to the clinic, asking questions and not liking my answers about adopting a War Dog," Mags said to Bauer, but turned back to the gunman. "I've just had it with you." She took a step toward him, and he seemed surprised. Before anybody had a chance to react, she had whacked him hard in the face. The gunman bolted backward, still holding the gun, pissed off, and sputtering.

She glared at him, her hands on her hips. "How dare you?" she said, with no intent of stopping her assault, even in the face of a gun. "You've been nothing but a pain in my ass for days, if not weeks now. And for what?" She was spitting mad. Only as she took another step forward, and the stranger pointed the gun directly at her, did she realize who really had the upper hand here. Still she shook her head at him. "No, this is bullshit. So unless you're prepared to go to jail for first-degree murder, you better put down that fucking gun."

"I'm not putting the gun down," he spat, his voice deadly. "That dog needs to die."

"Why?" Bauer asked, turning to look at him. "Because he killed somebody, somebody you care about?"

"He didn't kill anyone," he replied, with a sneer. "You don't understand anything."

"I don't understand because you haven't explained anything," Bauer said.

Mags added, "You've been so hell-bent on destroying my business and my life, even trying to burn down my house. And I want to know why. How the hell could anybody else understand what's going on in your brain?" She glared at him, as she looked over at the weary dog. "Toby, go inside."

"There he is." The gunman moved to point the gun toward Toby, who just looked at him. The gunman's lips curled a bit, but there was much less heat.

"You blame Toby, don't you?" Bauer asked. "For Ken's condition."

At that, the gunman turned and looked at him, clearly startled. "What?"

She looked from Bauer to the gunman and back. "Is that what this is about? Because of what happened to Ken?"

Glenn just stared at her, confused, as if not really sure how to answer that.

"This dog didn't cause Ken's health problems," she declared. "I know that for a fact because I've seen Ken's medical records. Toby wasn't anywhere close to your friend at the time of the explosion. Plus Toby's also way too young. He wasn't alive when Ken had his accident."

At that, the gunman's lips curled.

She shook her hand. "No, no, no. You don't get to do that now. This isn't about you. This is about what you're trying to do to this dog. And the people you're trying to annihilate in the process," she said, glaring at him. "This dog did nothing to you and did nothing to Ken."

"But he will," the gunman declared. "He didn't do his job."

At that, she turned and frowned at Bauer. "Do you know what he's talking about?"

Bauer looked at the gunman and slowly nodded. "I think I do." Bauer took a step toward Glenn. "That's what happened to Ken, isn't it? He was blown up from an IED, and a bomb-sniffing dog was supposedly out there to find them, making it safe for you guys."

The gunman nodded. "The fucking dog failed."

"I'm pretty darn sure that if a dog failed that day, it already paid the supreme price," Bauer noted. "That dog died that day. And you also know that the enemy is getting trickier all the time, always trying to make things harder for the dogs to find this stuff. So blaming a dog who died trying to do its job isn't fair, and blaming any other dog won't wash at all. These War Dogs don't even have a choice in the matter. They don't get to say, 'Hey, I'm not feeling like doing this today,' or, 'Hey, I'm trying here, but you guys aren't listening.' The War Dogs don't have a choice. Neither do the military guys. Ken was sent out to do his job, and he himself got injured. Why the hell would you blame a War Dog for the failure of man?"

From beside him, Mags added, "Because he doesn't have a man he can blame. That's it, isn't it? There's no one, no living person who you can blame, so the War Dogs became your target."

"That, and any other animal that's injured," Bauer added.

"If they're injured, they shouldn't be out there. It's kindness to put them down," Glenn stated but with a casual disregard in his tone.

Mags shook her head, glaring at the gunman still. "Doesn't seem to have started that way with you. I think you hated animals anyway, since forever, and this just allows you to vent all that anger in your world, … the anger for what happened to you and for what happened to your friend Ken. You think that accident has given you a license to go out and be an asshole to all animals," she snapped.

His face hardened. "You need to shut your mouth."

"Yeah?" She shook her head, giving him a sneer. "It won't be because of you."

He frowned at her. "Why the hell are you not scared? Do you not see the gun I have on you?"

"Pieces of shit like you are everywhere, and I've been hurt by some of the best. So kill me if you must, but I refuse to let assholes like you run my life for another minute."

He glared at her. "You don't know anything about me."

"I know that you're a coward," she declared, taking another step closer. "I know that you pick on animals that can't fight back. I know you hurt for your friend but because you can't help him, yet you're out here killing for him. But that's not what Ken wants. He loves dogs, this one included."

"He can't have it."

"Why? It would make him happy, wouldn't it?"

"No. It would just bring back all the memories."

"The memories of what?" Bauer asked. "The memories of what happened to him. Was he with a War Dog when it happened?"

Glenn nodded. "Yeah, and I don't want that to happen."

"Why don't you want him to relive what happened to

him?" Bauer asked, studying their gunman carefully. "Could it be that you're the one responsible for what happened to Ken and that you don't want him to remember?"

This started Glenn once again, and Bauer nodded. "That's it, isn't it? You were probably driving, and a War Dog had cleared the area. Were you driving?"

"No, I was in the second vehicle. Ken was supposed to ride with me, but I was pissed off at him, so I forced him to go in the first truck. The road had been cleared by a dog, but they drove over an IED anyway."

"So, you figure you're to blame."

"I am to blame," he cried out. "It's not fair. I was supposed to be the driver, so I should be dead, and he should be fine."

"Why?" Bauer prodded.

"Because I traded places with him," he snapped. "I didn't like anything about the situation, and I put him in danger, and look what happened to him."

"So, you don't want him to find out because he's the only friend you've got, isn't he?" Mags asked.

He stared at her. "I have other friends."

"No, you don't," she argued. "You're so full of anger and hatred and guilt that you don't have any friends. And now you're afraid that, if this War Dog brings back Ken's memories, you'll lose the only friend you do have."

"He was always the gentlest of souls," the gunman said. "We always wondered how he even made it through basic training. He was just so soft, and, once you got to know him, you understood that he was just all heart. I'm not surprised that he ended up the way he did," the gunman explained. "He was just one of those guys who had so much heart that you knew he should be protected."

"He's happy right now, isn't he?" Mags asked.

He nodded. "I don't get it. He doesn't remember anything."

"No, because he's got brain damage, and maybe that's a gift in a way."

"Maybe, but they told him that it could come back anytime and that something could trigger it."

"So, what then? You'll just kill every dog that comes near him?"

"It's not all dogs," he clarified. "But this one? ... It was a War Dog, like this one."

"Did he have a dog?"

"No, he didn't work them, but he was always around them. They loved him, of course, just like he loved them," he muttered. "I knew that this dog would be the one, and I wouldn't be able to keep Ken from finding out what had happened."

Mags nodded. "And you couldn't stand the thought of being alone, could you? You couldn't stand the guilt over what you did or couldn't take the chance of him finding out. Don't you think Ken's heart is big enough to forgive you?"

He stared at her. "How could anybody's heart be that big?" he asked. "There is no forgiving something like that. I was pissed off at him. I did it on purpose, but I didn't know the truck would blow up. But I did know, if they drove on the shoulder, there would be a bigger chance of an accident."

"So, that's what you told him to do?"

"Yeah. I told him that he had to go on the side because that's where the dog had cleared it."

"Jeez," Bauer muttered. "You know on those roads that's almost a death sentence."

He nodded slowly. "I did know it," he admitted, the

shame evident in his tone. "Afterward, there was nothing I could do. It was too late."

At that, she looked over at Bauer to see him studying the gunman, like he was some sort of insect. And he did think of him that way. As something to be studied by the specialists looking into how perverse and unkind the world could be, to pair somebody with a big heart with somebody like this.

She returned her attention to the gunman. "So, when you came back stateside, you found Ken?"

"He recognized me right away," he murmured. "I haven't had much luck holding friendships," he admitted, looking over at her and then dropping his gaze to the ground. "Yet he never judged me. He was just happy to have me back in his life."

"Except, with a simple flip of his memory, you could lose it all."

He nodded. "I've been so afraid. Just so much anger is inside me. When I see an injured or hurting animal, I just have to put it out of its misery."

"So, it's not so much that you kill them on purpose, but that you don't want them to suffer?" Mags asked.

"I don't know," he admitted. "I would like to say that, but sometimes it feels so damn good to know that they're dead, and I'm not."

"Back to the guilt again," Bauer stated.

"Is that guilt?" the gunman asked, with a harsh laugh. "It doesn't feel like it. It feels like something so much worse."

"Of course it does," Bauer agreed. "Have you gotten any therapy since you've come back?"

He shrugged. "There is no therapy if you're not blown up, if you're not in hard straits, you know? I came home at the end of my tour, and it's like, *you're done, bye, see you later.*"

"Why did you quit then?" Bauer asked.

He shrugged. "Because I needed to. Because it was starting to come out, ... out there. I was starting to be one of *those* guys."

At that, Bauer winced. "Right. Thank God you made that choice in time, but somehow you took a wrong turn here in your civilian life."

"Because I can't lose him," he wailed desperately. "Don't you understand? I can't lose Ken."

"Ken doesn't want to lose you either," she said. "He really cares."

"Maybe." He turned and looked around. "I don't even know what I'm doing here right now." He ran his hands through his hair. "Man, I came here to kill the dog."

"And yet you've crossed the line in many other ways," Bauer pointed out.

"And yet it's not crossing the line," he declared, now looking over at Mags, with a bright light in his gaze.

"No, you don't get to claim crazy or PTSD or anything else like that," she declared. "You're as sane as I am."

He glared at her, and she nodded. "I can see the way your brain is working, but it won't work with me."

"I could just pop you both, and nobody would ever know," he said, with a laugh.

"Oh, everybody would know," Bauer stated. "You think we haven't got this place rigged with cameras?"

"I'll light it all up. I'll set it on fire, burn down the damn house," he stated madly. "That'll take care of that."

"It's already live feeding," Bauer shared. "And the cops already know who you are, what you're doing, and that you're here," he shared. "Not to mention the fact that two people from my team, you probably haven't seen them, but they're already moving toward you."

He looked around. "You're just bullshitting me. You may know something about the military, but everybody was always playing games and pulling shit. It was all fun and games, until it wasn't."

"You mean, it was all fun and games, when it wasn't *you* who was hit by the IED," she clarified. "You're the kind of guy who makes everybody else's military experience a nightmare."

He shrugged. "Yeah, I was that kind of a guy, until I got my friend hurt and everybody else killed."

At that, Bauer winced. "More people were in the vehicle?"

"Yeah. Three others," he said.

"They all died?"

Glenn nodded. "But you know, I don't think about them half as much as I think about Ken."

"That's because you're invested in Ken and in what happens if Ken remembers," she pointed out. "The others are dead and gone, and they can't tattle. But, with Ken alive, you know you have something to lose. Yet I don't even know that Ken will ever remember."

"Nobody knows," he said harshly. "Yet I'm constantly aware of that possibility. I live in fear of that happening."

"That's interesting," she noted. "So what then? You can't kill every War Dog around. How the hell did you even hear about this one anyway?"

"One of the guys at the home saw it on the road. He stopped to help, but somebody was already picking it up, so he could take it to the vet for care. And, once he mentioned the War Dog to Ken, there was no talking to Ken about anything else. He just wanted to see it. He wanted to save it. As far as he was concerned, it was his dog, and everybody else needed to just let him look after it." The gunman shook his head. "Even trying to talk to him to help him understand that he couldn't just go get the dog was impossible. Every argument I made didn't convince Ken that it would be that same War Dog that he loved so much from over there."

Bauer nodded. "That's too bad because it's as if he's caught in that time loop, and that's probably one of the only memories he has from back then."

The gunman nodded. "That's the weird thing. He remembers the dog, but he doesn't remember much else."

"Except you."

Glenn nodded again. "He remembers me, and he remembers the dog," he corrected. "But if he remembers those two things, he could remember a lot more."

"He could," Mags agreed, "but maybe he never will. This wasn't the first time, was it, that you've killed a dog? And now Ken has to deal with what happens to you after this."

"Nothing will happen to me," he snapped, as he took several steps back, "because nobody will know."

"Really?" she asked, with a note of disbelief. "I get that you're trying to shoot the dog, but why do you feel you get to shoot me too?"

He shrugged. "No choice. It's all about self-preservation. Now move out of the way, so I can find the dog."

"I sent him inside," Bauer replied casually.

"No, you didn't. I would have heard that."

"It's a War Dog, remember?"

And then the gunman realized the power and the skills that Toby had.

Mags saw as Toby silently came up on the other side of the truck. He was hunched down low and had his lip curled. But, so far, he hadn't made a move, hadn't made a noise. Injured as he was, he was better, but, by the looks of it, he certainly wasn't ready to take on somebody like their gunman, who was more than prepared to kill Toby just because he existed.

"I really don't want you killing the War Dog," Bauer stated. "We've put a lot of time and effort into getting him healed and keeping him safe."

"That's nice," Glenn snarled, "like I give a shit."

"By the way, was it you who kidnapped the dog?" she asked suddenly. "From the clinic?"

"Ken called me from the highway to say his truck had broken down and that he needed help."

"But he doesn't drive," Bauer argued.

"Yeah, he does drive," the gunman stated. "That's something else that he can do, but he doesn't have wheels."

"So what? He just went out and got a car?" Bauer asked.

Again the gunman laughed. "Exactly. He was really good at boosting cars back then, yet another Uncle Sam trait that he was trained to do."

"So, he steals a car," Bauer figures, "then he comes down and breaks into the clinic and takes the dog. Then the vehicle breaks down, so Ken calls you for help. And, when you get there, you see the dog and what? You try to shoot it?"

"Ken's back was turned, and he was trying to get his stuff moved into my car. I shot at the dog, and it took off, then all hell broke loose. I've been trying to find the damn thing ever since, and so has Ken."

"Of course because, in his mind, he was trying to rescue

it, but because you stopped by, and the dog got away, Ken doesn't know what happened. He's caught in another time loop."

"Maybe so, but once it's dead, I can just tell him that it was old and that it died."

"You think that'll be the end of it?" Mags asked.

"Sure, he'll believe me." At that, Glenn turned and looked around. "Where the fuck is the goddamn dog?"

"I sent him inside. I told you that," Bauer repeated. He took two steps toward him, but the gun came up in his face.

"Don't move."

"Once again you're back to that decision-making point," Bauer declared. "Do you want to spend the rest of your life in jail for shooting us?"

"Maybe. At least then I'd be a hero in Ken's eyes."

"How do you figure that?" Bauer asked.

"Because I'll kill the dog and tell Ken that I was trying to save him, but you're the one who stopped me."

"Wow," she replied, "you're really all about *you*, aren't you?"

"Everybody is all about themselves, and when they tell you that they're not, … they're lying."

She winced. "I've kind of come to that conclusion myself, but we don't have to be assholes about it."

When Bauer looked over at her curiously, she shrugged. "I just did some thinking while you were gone, that's all."

"Good thinking?" he asked curiously.

She flashed him a bright smile. "Maybe, but we have to get out of this scenario first."

Glenn yelled out, "Hello? Man with the gun here. Cut the chitchat."

AT THAT, BAUER laughed at Mags's comment. "If you're thinking about what I'm thinking about, I am so on it." And, with that, he turned back to the gunman, took another two steps toward him, and when the gun started back up again, he knew it was time. He jumped and, with a kick, knocked the gun free and, with his right hand, punched Glenn hard in the jaw.

The gunman dropped, then tried to scramble back up, but Toby was right there, his jaw clamped hard on Glenn's shoulder, holding him down. Glenn started screaming.

Bauer turned to Mags. "Got any zip ties?"

She looked over at Toby. "Sure, but can you get Toby to release him?"

"I will, but we need to secure Glenn first. What, are you worried about this guy?"

"No," she snapped, looking at Bauer as if he were crazy. "I'm worried about Toby." With that she bolted inside.

Once she returned and Bauer tied up Glenn's hands and feet, it didn't take much to get Toby to release Glenn. Bauer smiled at Toby and said, "You have no idea how good your life is about to get, buddy."

The gunman was writhing beneath Bauer, still making far too much noise. Bauer gave him a good shake, grabbing the shoulder Toby had just released for emphasis. "Stay down and shut up already, will you?"

And, with that, he pulled out his phone. He looked up just in time to see Badger getting out of a vehicle. "You missed all the fun," Bauer called out.

Badger nodded. "Looks like it. Cops are on the way."

"How did you know?" she asked, walking closer.

"The cameras. It was all on the live feed."

She looked at Bauer and asked, "You were serious?"

He nodded. "I told you that I wouldn't let anything happen to you." Then he stood up and added, "Now maybe you'll trust me."

And, when he opened his arms, she raced into them.

CHAPTER 13

B Y THE TIME they finally closed the door on the last of their *guests*, Mags turned and looked at Bauer, then leaned back against the door. "Good God almighty."

He smiled, then walked over and pulled her into his arms and held her. "The great news is that it's over."

She burrowed closer, giving in to finally feeling the sense of relief she hadn't been able to while the cops, the gunman, and even Badger were still here. Glenn had talked to them some, explained a little bit more, and finally had been led away by the cops. Some stayed behind to take Mags's and Bauer's statements, which seemed to take forever. Badger had left in the middle of that. Finally the last of the police had left, and Mags was alone with Bauer.

She looked down at Toby, who was crashed on the floor beside them. "Do you think Badger will have a problem letting me keep him?"

"I don't think so. Did you mention it to him?"

She shook her head. "I didn't even think about it, not with everything else going on. Wow, what a day."

"It was, but it's all good. We now have the answers, and the culprit has been caught."

She smiled at him. "Suddenly I'm really hungry. Are you?"

He laughed at that. "Yes, but I hope you don't mind

reheated Chinese food."

She groaned, then shrugged. "I often microwave leftovers anyway, and they are fine. At this point in time, I really don't care."

"Good, I'll grab them, and let's go eat." He retrieved the to-go bag from his vehicle and then led the way into the kitchen.

When she looked at the spread that he'd bought, she stared. "You know, with all this, we could have fed everyone, while we gave our statements."

"I suppose, but I had no intention of starving myself tonight." He was dishing up Toby some food and gave him fresh water as well.

She agreed with him, but, at the same time, he'd chosen quite a spread of various entrees and sides. They each quickly served themselves a plate, then popped them into the microwave and sat down at the kitchen table. She started in and ate steadily.

When he reached a hand across to hers, she looked up at him.

"You better slow down, before you make yourself sick."

Her shoulders slumped, and she looked down at the food. "Good call. I wasn't even thinking. I'm just so tired, yet so hungry."

"A good tired, I'll bet."

She laughed. "It is." She sat back, noting that, with the first wave of hunger appeased, she was much calmer. "It's just been hard, you know? While you're in it, you're just trying to get through it and don't even realize how much it impacts you, what that does to a person. Especially when it goes on and on like it did."

"No, you don't. Not until it's you," he added, with a

smile. "And now that you've had that kind of experience, hopefully you won't ever have to go through such a thing again."

"That would make me very happy. It definitely isn't something I want to deal with."

"No, I'm sure it isn't." By the time they finished, she was much more mellow. He brought out a bottle of wine. "I found this in the back of the cupboard. Any reason we shouldn't open it?"

She didn't even know she had this wine, then shrugged and said, "I don't know where it came from."

He popped the cork. "I'm not sure it goes with Chinese takeout, but we're more or less finished eating anyway. I thought maybe it would help you unwind."

She nodded. "The perfect touch at the end of the day." Then she yawned.

He looked at her. "Sounds like you're ready for bed."

"Not yet, it's too early." She glanced down at her phone and smiled. "Way too early."

"Let's go sit out on the deck then," he suggested. After taking care of the dishes and putting away the extra food, they moved out to the deck. "We can eat some of that later."

"I won't be eating anything later. I'm stuffed."

He nodded. "Tomorrow then."

Out on the deck, she crashed on one of the big loungers and felt everything inside her just melting. "The wine is the perfect touch," she muttered. "I hadn't realized how much all the stress and tension had me knotted up."

"It's good that it's finally easing up now, right?"

"I know. With a good night's sleep, I'll be good as new," she said brightly.

"Perfect. Then we can talk about what comes next."

"And what does come next?" she asked, looking startled.

He shrugged. "I'm sure the cops will have more questions, and we'll be dealing with all that stuff for a while."

She winced. "Glenn probably won't plead not guilty to any of this."

"That's not the point. Besides, by the time Glenn gets a lawyer, the lawyer will insist he plead not guilty, at least at first." Bauer shrugged. "But it's not as if we don't have a ton of evidence. The authorities have copies of all the video, and Glenn can be seen quite plainly in all of it. They've got all of our statements about all that he did and said tonight. So, with any luck, his conviction should go pretty smoothly. He'll probably end up taking a plea for a lesser sentence."

"I hope so," she stated. "I can't say I really want to go through a trial on all this."

"No, but, if it's necessary, we will," Bauer stated, his tone firm.

She looked over at him. "Maybe tomorrow I'll talk to Badger about keeping Toby," she shared. "I did talk to Kat earlier. She called about possibly making a prosthetic for Toby. Thank you for that."

He raised his eyebrows and shrugged. "No need to thank me. You mentioned it, and all I did was relay the message. She would have done it, if you'd asked her."

"Maybe, but it just reminded me that you are one of the good guys in life."

He laughed. "Why? Because I care about dogs?" he asked affectionately.

"Absolutely. I've had a lot of epiphanies today," she murmured. "One involved the realization that I hadn't done as well by the animals as I could have. I used to take in a lot of foster animals before. I used to work hard to heal them up and to get them socialized and even trained a bit, then get them fostered or adopted out to permanent homes. Somewhere around the same time that I got so badly hurt ..."

"The marriage?"

"Yeah. I shut down the foster work," she murmured. "I don't really have any excuse for it. It was just one of those things, I guess. ... All of a sudden, I couldn't handle the hurt anymore. I just stopped dealing with it. Now, having Toby around and wanting him so badly reminded me of all the things I'd given up in order to live in my little glass castle," she shared.

He nodded. "I've had a similar epiphany myself. That's why I turned down your offer earlier today."

She looked over at him, smiled, and said, "That really surprised me."

"Yeah, honest to God, I surprised myself."

She burst out laughing at that, while he grinned at her. "I didn't think a guy had that in him."

"Hey now, we're not all sex maniacs."

"No, you're not," she stated, with an eye roll.

He smiled. "I saw something in you, and I realized that I really wanted more. And I just didn't want to shortchange what could be a really beautiful future." He reached a hand across, and she placed hers in it.

"That was part of my realization today. I want that future too," she murmured.

He stared at her, his fingers tightening. "So, what does that mean?"

"It means that I think we have something very special. ... I think we have something we should be rejoicing in and not fighting over."

"Oh, I agree with that," he stated.

"I want to see where it takes us."

He grinned. "You're sitting awfully far away for that."

"For what?" she teased, batting her lashes at him, as she tossed back the rest of her wine. Putting her glass down carefully, she stood and moved over to his lounger and sat on his lap. "Now this is nice," she muttered, as she nestled against his shoulder.

"It is, but it would be so much nicer if we were upstairs in bed."

"Oh, I don't know about that," she noted. "I got turned down in that department today, so I might still be stinging with rejection."

He chuckled. "No, you're not, but you did realize what's important and what we could have, so there's an awful lot in there for both of us to unpack."

"I know. It's been a tough few days."

"Worth it though," he replied. "Look where we're at now."

She tilted her head back and looked up at him. "What if it doesn't last?"

He placed a finger against her lips. "What if it does?"

She frowned, then she nodded. "I guess it's up to us to see that we make it go the distance."

"Exactly," he agreed. "I don't know about you, but I'm really looking forward to it."

She chuckled. "Yeah, me too." She smiled, as she studied him. "I didn't think I would ever get to this point again."

"I hear you there. I went through that as well, but, when you see something that you really, really want, and you know how powerful that feeling is, it makes you realize that today is what is important, not holding on to the hurts of the past."

"You're a very wise person," she said. "I don't think I would have gotten to this point quite so easily without you."

"I think it's the combination of the two of us," he suggested, as he tapped her on the nose. "This isn't something either of us could find with just anybody, or it would have happened by now."

"I hope not. I would like to think it's special."

"It is special," he declared, then grinned at her. "No way it's not. I mean, just look at all the people we've each met over the last many years. We didn't get into a relationship with any of them."

She nodded. "I've never met anybody quite like you."

"Exactly," he agreed, "and I've never met anybody quite like you. So, as much as I hate to admit it, Kat and Badger were right."

She laughed at that. "I did bring it up with them today. With Kat at least. She told me that there was no pressure and what I really needed to do was just talk to you and sort it out."

"She was right about that, and I hope that, anytime you've got something you need to talk out, you'll come to me."

"I will," she said. "That was just, you know, girl talk."

"Ah, girl talk."

"Absolutely." She looked up at him and smiled. "Besides, she fully approves."

He nodded. "I got that impression from Badger too." He returned her smile.

"I really like them. I'm glad that we'll be nearby."

"You are for sure," he said. "I still have to figure out what I'm doing for a living."

"I wanted to ask you about that and then I thought, you

know what? It doesn't matter, as long as you are happy with what you do." She felt his reaction to this, and she nodded. "I know for a lot of people a certain career matters, but you know what? You do you."

"I'm glad to hear that," he replied. "I am looking at options, maybe something involving security, but I'm looking at all kinds of things. One thing I wouldn't mind doing is fostering animals, you know? Maybe help to rehabilitate them and to find them new homes."

"Oh, I can get behind that," she declared. "If you don't do anything but that, it would be very worthwhile. I was thinking about doing more of that again myself, but solo? I've never been able to do it on a very large scale."

"It would definitely be worthwhile, but that venture costs money, and it doesn't bring any in."

She shrugged. "I've got plenty of space on this property. Plus I have money."

"So do I," he replied. "I just don't tell people about it."

She looked up at him, then smiled. "In that case, it sounds like we're all set."

He chuckled. "Besides, you might need a hand or two at the clinic every once in a while."

"I'm always happy to have help there," she noted. "The animals always need something. Even if it's just a cuddle."

"There's no such thing as *just a cuddle*," he pointed out, pulling her tighter into his arms. "We all need cuddles."

"For a long time I was pretty sure I didn't. But, being in your arms like this, it reminds me of what I've been missing."

"That's why I didn't want what we have to be something flashy and fast," he explained. "I wanted it to be savored, nurtured, cherished."

She frowned up at him and asked, "Does that mean you're expecting our first time together to be slow?" She arched one eyebrow.

"I didn't say that," he clarified. "In fact, I suspect it will be hard and fast. Then we'll get to the slow and easy afterward."

"Oh, so you think you're good for two times, are you?" she asked, winding her arms around his neck. "An awful lot of talk for somebody who hasn't done any showing yet."

He leaned over, kissed her gently, and muttered, "In that case, I suggest we take this upstairs. Unless you're planning on making love outside."

She thought about it, thought about what they'd been through, and made a decision. "Not today. Tomorrow perhaps. You know that sense of being watched is something that'll take a while to get over."

"Maybe you never will," he noted. Then he shifted, so she had her feet on the deck. She stood up, wondering what he was up to, as he hopped to his feet, wrapped an arm around her shoulders, and added, "Let's take care of everything down here, and then we can go up."

"Sounds good to me," she said.

They walked through the house to confirm everything was good, took Toby out to pee, set the alarm, and then headed upstairs. "I really need sleep tonight," Mags muttered.

"I know," he said gently. "Tomorrow is Sunday though, so that will help."

"You're right," she said in hope, "and there aren't any animals at the clinic, so I get a whole day to stay in bed if I want to." He stopped, waggled his eyebrows, and she burst out laughing. "And, as a bonus, we have plenty of Chinese food left," she added.

"I know."

Something in his tone had her staring at him. "Oh my God, that's why you bought so much, isn't it? You scoundrel!"

He laughed. "Let's just say that I was hoping for that."

She couldn't believe it. "So you must have been very sure that I would come around to your way of thinking."

"No, but I know a very smart woman when I see one, so I had faith." At the doorway to her bedroom, he pulled her into his arms. "Unless you have some objection to that."

"No, it just shows a level of deviousness I wasn't expecting." She chuckled.

"No, not devious, *practical*," he clarified, with a note of protest. "You can bet your ass that was definitely some good old Boy Scout preparedness."

She burst out laughing at that, wrapped her arms around his neck, and asked, "Yeah? And what else are you prepared for, Boy Scout?"

He chuckled, picked her up in his arms, and carried her a few steps to the bed to gently toss her there. "Let's just say we have the whole night to figure it out." She opened up her arms, and he slowly came down beside her. "I just want to make sure you know what you're in for."

"I know what I'm in for," she stated, sitting up, pulling her T-shirt over her head, and tossing it onto the ground. "Do you?"

And, with that, she quickly stripped off the rest of her clothes. Before he had a chance to do anything else, she straddled him, as he sat on the edge of the bed. She noted, "Maybe you're the one that needs a little adjustment time."

He nodded. "Absolutely, so you'll be gentle with me,

won't you?"

She gave him a deep gaze and shook her head. "Probably not."

He burst out laughing and leaned flat on the bed with a big grin, as she came down on top of him and whispered, "You're wearing way too many clothes."

"But you're on top of me now, so I can hardly get my clothes off."

"You'll just have to struggle through it," she teased. She put her hands on his belt and quickly unbuckled it, then unzipped his jeans. When she slipped a hand inside, he bolted upright again, glaring down at her. "That's not fair."

"Hey, all is fair in love and war," she stated, as she stood up and pulled his T-shirt over his head. Laughing, they finally got him undressed.

She pulled him into her arms, and he asked, "Absolutely no comment?"

"You're beautiful, so what the hell more can there be?"

And, with that, she expertly pulled off his prosthetic and pushed him back on the bed, coming down on top of him. He looked at her in wonder, as she smiled at him. "You think I haven't seen worse? They may not have come from war wounds, but believe me. I've seen injuries from hell."

His face softened. "You're a special woman to be helping so many animals."

"I don't know about that. Some days I don't know if I can do it, and then I just get up the next day and keep going forward."

"That's all any of us can do," he said. "We're periodically tested. Sometimes we're good, and sometimes we struggle, but if we just take it all one day at a time, we'll get through. Hopefully having somebody with us will make the journey a whole lot less painful." Then he rolled over, pulled her into his arms, and said, "And now, neither of us is alone anymore."

He lowered his head, and he kissed her, his passion driving deep into her toes. She wrapped her thighs around him, as he pushed her hips up tight against him, and she whispered, "You're right. First time hard and fast."

Before she even had a chance to understand how intense this would be, he took her on a ride that left her gasping for more. When she came apart in his arms before he had even entered her, she was spent. When she lay here, tears rolling down her face, he asked, "Are you okay?"

She nodded. "Yes, really okay. I hadn't realized just how long it had been."

"It won't be any longer." And, with that, he dove into the heart of her. She stilled, feeling the complete possession, that sense of stretching, that sense of ownership, and she welcomed every last bit of it.

Then she finally looked up at him and whispered, "Now move."

He smiled and started to plunge deep. First, second, third, and by the time he hit the fourth, she was coming apart again, and by the fifth, he was shoved deep inside, and it was his turn.

Just feeling his climax deep inside had her exploding again and then again.

By the time she finally calmed down in his arms, he whispered, "Wow."

"No, that's my line," she countered. "*Wow* doesn't do it justice though."

He pulled her into his arms and said, "After that, I think you need to sleep."

"I don't want to sleep," she whispered, but already she was yawning.

"You might not want to, sweetheart, but it's definitely what you need."

She looked up at him and asked, "Will you be here when I wake up?"

He nodded, then dropped a kiss on her temple, and declared, "Absolutely. Today and every other day."

And, with that promise, she closed her eyes and fell asleep.

Life would be much more beautiful with him.

EPILOGUE

B ADGER WALKED INTO the dining room, finding his wife, Kat, sorting papers into folders. He stopped, his hands on his hips, and stared at the documents, but, upside down, he couldn't read clearly what they were.

When she looked up, she gave him a smile and said, "More work."

"What kind of work?"

She chuckled. "Four more K9 files."

His eyebrows shot up. "Seriously?"

"Yes, they just came in this morning. Commander Cross did phone ahead of time, and he asked if we were up for it. Of course I said yes, and he was extremely grateful."

Badger added, "We have had amazing successes in doing this War Dog work."

"Commander Cross has also told several other people in his department how well we have done with it all. I guess we've made a name for ourselves, without expecting to."

Badger rolled his eyes at that. "Not sure that's a good thing."

"Of course it is," Kat said, with a laugh. "Anything that we do to help these animals and to give the department other options for helping these War Dogs is a good thing." She tapped the file closest to her and then slid it toward him.

Badger shook his head. "We're out of men."

"Nope." Kat laughed. "I know that you think so, but I also know that each dog has a rescue out there. And it's important we find the right ones to pair up with each War Dog."

"I agree," Badger murmured, "but that doesn't change the fact that we have nobody to call on for help right now."

"I'm not so sure about that," she said, as she slid the file to him again.

Badger looked down at the file and shrugged. "So, you have somebody in mind?"

"I do," she murmured. "I was thinking about somebody I was working with today. Delta has consistent ankle problems, and I've seen him regularly over the last couple months. However, we think we've got his ankle joint sorted. He has a lot more weight on the outside of his right leg than he has on the inside." Seeing the look on Badger's face, she laughed. "That's the technical stuff I've been dealing with for him. Just a pressure joint adjustment."

Badger smirked. "So that would be good, if Delta's ready."

"It would be, and I was talking to him. He absolutely loves dogs and was considering doing canine training, potentially to work in the police department or in some other capacity. And I mentioned how we had done all this work with the retired War Dogs coming out of the military, and he grew quite excited. He worked with several War Dogs while he was overseas and loved everything about it. He's a big fan of the department and what they were doing. Hated to see any kind of animal mistreated. And was a big advocate for the animals. He did a lot of first aid work on them as well."

"So he's a vet?" Badger asked.

"No, but he was a vet assistant, before he went into the military. He was contemplating going to veterinarian school, but I think just the amount of years involved was a deterrent for him back then, and particularly now with his health. However, he's getting better, and I would say he's probably fully capable of doing something like these War Dog cases."

Badger nodded. "Lots of years to invest in becoming a veterinarian, and Delta, with his military service, is now probably already in his late twenties or early thirties, right?"

"Delta's thirty-four, not married, not engaged, doesn't have any attachments."

Badger's eyebrows went up at that.

She nodded. "Of course I guess he had somebody, but she broke up with him when he was deployed." Badger frowned at that. She agreed. "I know that you and I have a hard time with that. However, a lot of people have been through that experience, and it hasn't stopped them. Delta's moving forward with his life."

Badger asked, "And did he say he would like to do something like this?"

Kat nodded. "I told him that, at the moment, we didn't have a War Dog file, but I would consider him, if I got one." Again she motioned at the table and the file she kept sliding toward Badger. "And that would be the file."

"And why this file? Why would Delta be the right man for this job? What about this case screams *Delta* to you?"

Kat nodded, as she pulled her chair away from the dining room table to situate it closer to Badger, where she relaxed, facing him. "Yes, Delta Granger is the man for this file."

"And that's his real name?"

"Yes, that's his real name."

"Okay, and what about this War Dog?" Badger asked.

"What matters is this dog was used as a comfort dog for the injured War Dogs."

He pulled out a dining room chair, sat down across from her, and studied her features. "Seriously? I didn't even know something like that was possible."

"It is, and it's not common, but it should be common in a vet clinic. If you have injured animals, another animal— particularly one of the same species—can often give comfort to the injured ones. So there was a military veterinarian on staff who used several comfort dogs to help with the injured animals. So this War Dog, now a comfort dog, whose name is Grace, was one of those. She was injured, and she's missing her back leg and tail, plus damaged the muscles in between." Kat looked at her own missing limb.

Badger couldn't help but stare down at his as well. "I can't even imagine what the pain would be for a dog to go through that. ... Of course, that would make Grace one of ours."

Kat chuckled. "It absolutely would."

"Well, I'm game if you and Delta are," he murmured. "You're a better determinant of character than I am."

"I'm not sure that is true," she murmured. "I might have luck in pairing relationships but not to the extent you do." She picked up her phone. "I'm going to call him. He was just here earlier today. In fact, you've met him. Remember the guy who did the patio stonework at Jager's?"

Badger smiled. "He did good work."

Kat chuckled, holding the phone to her ear. "He did do great work," she said, listening to it ring. "Delta, it's Kat. Can you come over tomorrow? Let's talk about something we might have available." She smiled, looking at Badger.

"The file just came in. … That would be great. Thank you."
She smiled as she ended the call. "He's coming tomorrow."

"Perfect," Badger murmured. "Now what's up for tonight?"

She laughed. "Our *kids* are coming over to enjoy the pool, as usual, maybe some barbecued steak."

He grabbed her hand, giving it a kiss. "With you, I'm game for anything."

This concludes Book 22 of The K9 Files: Bauer.
Read about Delta: The K9 Files, Book 23

The K9 Files: Delta (Book #23)

Welcome to the all new K9 Files series reconnecting readers with the unforgettable men from SEALs of Steel in a new series of action packed, page turning romantic suspense that fans have come to expect from USA TODAY Bestselling author Dale Mayer. Pssst… you'll meet other favorite characters from SEALs of Honor and Heroes for Hire too!

Delta is always eager to help animals in need, especially when the request comes from Kat and Badger. Learning the animal is a retired K9 dog, now serving as a comfort animal for other injured dogs, Delta's determination only increases. However, arriving in town, Delta's contact has now vanished, and Delta discovers the War Dog is missing as well. Although Delta had looked forward to dinner with the woman he'd spoken to frequently on the phone, he now finds himself entangled in a disconcerting theory that extends beyond just one War Dog.

Rebecca has always had a soft spot for animals, and retired War Dog Gracie has effortlessly found a place in her heart. However, Rebecca's attempts to adopt her from the center are consistently thwarted. As Rebecca seeks a solution, she stumbles upon something far more sinister, and soon realizes she is out of her depth.

All she can do is hope that Delta comes through for both her and Gracie … before it is too late.

Find Book 23 here!

To find out more visit Dale Mayer's website.

https://geni.us/DMSDelta

Author's Note

Thank you for reading Bauer: The K9 Files, Book 22! If you enjoyed the book, please take a moment and leave a short review.

Dear reader,

I love to hear from readers, and you can contact me at my website: www.dalemayer.com or at my Facebook author page. To be informed of new releases and special offers, sign up for my newsletter or follow me on BookBub. And if you are interested in joining Dale Mayer's Reader Group, here is the Facebook sign up page.
http://geni.us/DaleMayerFBGroup

Cheers,
Dale Mayer

About the Author

Dale Mayer is a *USA Today* best-selling author, best known for her SEALs military romances, her Psychic Visions series, and her Lovely Lethal Garden cozy series. Her contemporary romances are raw and full of passion and emotion (Broken But … Mending, Hathaway House series). Her thrillers will keep you guessing (Kate Morgan, By Death series), and her romantic comedies will keep you giggling (*It's a Dog's Life*, a stand-alone novella; and the Broken Protocols series, starring Charming Marvin, the cat).

Dale honors the stories that come to her—and some of them are crazy, break all the rules and cross multiple genres!

To go with her fiction, she also writes nonfiction in many different fields, with books available on résumé writing, companion gardening, and the US mortgage system. All her books are available in print and ebook format.

Connect with Dale Mayer Online

Dale's Website – www.dalemayer.com
Twitter – @DaleMayer
Facebook Page – geni.us/DaleMayerFBFanPage
Facebook Group – geni.us/DaleMayerFBGroup
BookBub – geni.us/DaleMayerBookbub
Instagram – geni.us/DaleMayerInstagram
Goodreads – geni.us/DaleMayerGoodreads
Newsletter – geni.us/DaleNews

Also by Dale Mayer

Published Adult Books:

Shadow Recon
Magnus, Book 1
Rogan, Book 2
Egan, Book 3
Barret, Book 4
Whalen, Book 5
Nikolai, Book 6

Bullard's Battle
Ryland's Reach, Book 1
Cain's Cross, Book 2
Eton's Escape, Book 3
Garret's Gambit, Book 4
Kano's Keep, Book 5
Fallon's Flaw, Book 6
Quinn's Quest, Book 7
Bullard's Beauty, Book 8
Bullard's Best, Book 9
Bullard's Battle, Books 1–2
Bullard's Battle, Books 3–4
Bullard's Battle, Books 5–6
Bullard's Battle, Books 7–8

Terkel's Team

Damon's Deal, Book 1
Wade's War, Book 2
Gage's Goal, Book 3
Calum's Contact, Book 4
Rick's Road, Book 5
Scott's Summit, Book 6
Brody's Beast, Book 7
Terkel's Twist, Book 8
Terkel's Triumph, Book 9

Terk's Guardians

Radar, Book 1
Legend, Book 2
Bojan, Book 3
Langdon, Book 4

Kate Morgan

Simon Says… Hide, Book 1
Simon Says… Jump, Book 2
Simon Says… Ride, Book 3
Simon Says… Scream, Book 4
Simon Says… Run, Book 5
Simon Says… Walk, Book 6
Simon Says… Forgive, Book 7
Simon Says… Swim, Book 8

Hathaway House

Aaron, Book 1
Brock, Book 2
Cole, Book 3
Denton, Book 4

The K9 Files

Rowan, Book 10
Caleb, Book 11
Kurt, Book 12
Tucker, Book 13
Harley, Book 14
Kyron, Book 15
Jenner, Book 16
Rhys, Book 17
Landon, Book 18
Harper, Book 19
Kascius, Book 20
Declan, Book 21
Bauer, Book 22
Delta, Book 23
The K9 Files, Books 1–2
The K9 Files, Books 3–4
The K9 Files, Books 5–6
The K9 Files, Books 7–8
The K9 Files, Books 9–10
The K9 Files, Books 11–12

Lovely Lethal Gardens

Arsenic in the Azaleas, Book 1
Bones in the Begonias, Book 2
Corpse in the Carnations, Book 3
Daggers in the Dahlias, Book 4
Evidence in the Echinacea, Book 5
Footprints in the Ferns, Book 6
Gun in the Gardenias, Book 7
Handcuffs in the Heather, Book 8
Ice Pick in the Ivy, Book 9
Jewels in the Juniper, Book 10

Killer in the Kiwis, Book 11
Lifeless in the Lilies, Book 12
Murder in the Marigolds, Book 13
Nabbed in the Nasturtiums, Book 14
Offed in the Orchids, Book 15
Poison in the Pansies, Book 16
Quarry in the Quince, Book 17
Revenge in the Roses, Book 18
Silenced in the Sunflowers, Book 19
Toes up in the Tulips, Book 20
Uzi in the Urn, Book 21
Victim in the Violets, Book 22
Whispers in the Wisteria, Book 23
Lovely Lethal Gardens, Books 1–2
Lovely Lethal Gardens, Books 3–4
Lovely Lethal Gardens, Books 5–6
Lovely Lethal Gardens, Books 7–8
Lovely Lethal Gardens, Books 9–10

Psychic Visions Series

Tuesday's Child
Hide 'n Go Seek
Maddy's Floor
Garden of Sorrow
Knock Knock...
Rare Find
Eyes to the Soul
Now You See Her
Shattered
Into the Abyss
Seeds of Malice
Eye of the Falcon

Itsy-Bitsy Spider
Unmasked
Deep Beneath
From the Ashes
Stroke of Death
Ice Maiden
Snap, Crackle…
What If…
Talking Bones
String of Tears
Inked Forever
Insanity
Psychic Visions Books 1–3
Psychic Visions Books 4–6
Psychic Visions Books 7–9

By Death Series
Touched by Death
Haunted by Death
Chilled by Death
By Death Books 1–3

Broken Protocols – Romantic Comedy Series
Cat's Meow
Cat's Pajamas
Cat's Cradle
Cat's Claus
Broken Protocols 1-4

Broken and… Mending
Skin
Scars

Scales (of Justice)
Broken but... Mending 1-3

Glory

Genesis
Tori
Celeste
Glory Trilogy

Biker Blues

Morgan: Biker Blues, Volume 1
Cash: Biker Blues, Volume 2

SEALs of Honor

Mason: SEALs of Honor, Book 1
Hawk: SEALs of Honor, Book 2
Dane: SEALs of Honor, Book 3
Swede: SEALs of Honor, Book 4
Shadow: SEALs of Honor, Book 5
Cooper: SEALs of Honor, Book 6
Markus: SEALs of Honor, Book 7
Evan: SEALs of Honor, Book 8
Mason's Wish: SEALs of Honor, Book 9
Chase: SEALs of Honor, Book 10
Brett: SEALs of Honor, Book 11
Devlin: SEALs of Honor, Book 12
Easton: SEALs of Honor, Book 13
Ryder: SEALs of Honor, Book 14
Macklin: SEALs of Honor, Book 15
Corey: SEALs of Honor, Book 16
Warrick: SEALs of Honor, Book 17
Tanner: SEALs of Honor, Book 18

Jackson: SEALs of Honor, Book 19

Kanen: SEALs of Honor, Book 20

Nelson: SEALs of Honor, Book 21

Taylor: SEALs of Honor, Book 22

Colton: SEALs of Honor, Book 23

Troy: SEALs of Honor, Book 24

Axel: SEALs of Honor, Book 25

Baylor: SEALs of Honor, Book 26

Hudson: SEALs of Honor, Book 27

Lachlan: SEALs of Honor, Book 28

Paxton: SEALs of Honor, Book 29

Bronson: SEALs of Honor, Book 30

Hale: SEALs of Honor, Book 31

SEALs of Honor, Books 1–3

SEALs of Honor, Books 4–6

SEALs of Honor, Books 7–10

SEALs of Honor, Books 11–13

SEALs of Honor, Books 14–16

SEALs of Honor, Books 17–19

SEALs of Honor, Books 20–22

SEALs of Honor, Books 23–25

Heroes for Hire

Levi's Legend: Heroes for Hire, Book 1

Stone's Surrender: Heroes for Hire, Book 2

Merk's Mistake: Heroes for Hire, Book 3

Rhodes's Reward: Heroes for Hire, Book 4

Flynn's Firecracker: Heroes for Hire, Book 5

Logan's Light: Heroes for Hire, Book 6

Harrison's Heart: Heroes for Hire, Book 7

Saul's Sweetheart: Heroes for Hire, Book 8

Dakota's Delight: Heroes for Hire, Book 9

SEALs of Steel

Cade: SEALs of Steel, Book 3
Talon: SEALs of Steel, Book 4
Laszlo: SEALs of Steel, Book 5
Geir: SEALs of Steel, Book 6
Jager: SEALs of Steel, Book 7
The Final Reveal: SEALs of Steel, Book 8
SEALs of Steel, Books 1–4
SEALs of Steel, Books 5–8
SEALs of Steel, Books 1–8

The Mavericks

Kerrick, Book 1
Griffin, Book 2
Jax, Book 3
Beau, Book 4
Asher, Book 5
Ryker, Book 6
Miles, Book 7
Nico, Book 8
Keane, Book 9
Lennox, Book 10
Gavin, Book 11
Shane, Book 12
Diesel, Book 13
Jerricho, Book 14
Killian, Book 15
Hatch, Book 16
Corbin, Book 17
Aiden, Book 18
The Mavericks, Books 1–2
The Mavericks, Books 3–4
The Mavericks, Books 5–6

The Mavericks, Books 7–8
The Mavericks, Books 9–10
The Mavericks, Books 11–12

Standalone Novellas
It's a Dog's Life
Riana's Revenge
Second Chances

Published Young Adult Books:

Family Blood Ties Series
Vampire in Denial
Vampire in Distress
Vampire in Design
Vampire in Deceit
Vampire in Defiance
Vampire in Conflict
Vampire in Chaos
Vampire in Crisis
Vampire in Control
Vampire in Charge
Family Blood Ties Set 1–3
Family Blood Ties Set 1–5
Family Blood Ties Set 4–6
Family Blood Ties Set 7–9
Sian's Solution, A Family Blood Ties Series Prequel
    Novelette

Design series
Dangerous Designs
Deadly Designs

Darkest Designs
Design Series Trilogy

Standalone
In Cassie's Corner
Gem Stone (a Gemma Stone Mystery)
Time Thieves

Published Non-Fiction Books:

Career Essentials
Career Essentials: The Résumé
Career Essentials: The Cover Letter
Career Essentials: The Interview
Career Essentials: 3 in 1